THE
FEEDING
GROUNDS

THE
FEEDING
GROUNDS

BL BLAKE

authorHOUSE®

AuthorHouse™ LLC
1663 Liberty Drive
Bloomington, IN 47403
www.authorhouse.com
Phone: 1-800-839-8640

Published by AuthorHouse   08/24/2013

ISBN: 978-1-4918-0373-8 (sc)
ISBN: 978-1-4918-0374-5 (e)

Library of Congress Control Number: 2013913992

CHAPTER 1

6:32 AM:

A single shark swam in from the open ocean toward the beach. He was hungry and looking for something to eat. His massive prehistoric body moved steadily in the sea just as his ancestors had done for millions of years. His force in the water caused all the other creatures to move out of his way. In his wake a queer silence penetrated the ocean. The shark did not think, it only ate. With the efficiently that million of years of development had produced, this animal ruled the world of ocean.

As the shark approached the land below the cliffs of Santa Barbara, his massive body turned and swam south until he was some fifty feet from the shore. The shark followed the shoreline. Near West Beach the shark saw a single seal lying on its back in the near darkness of the early morning surf. The shark swam on.

Following the shoreline there were large boulders and a jetty of cement which cut off the ocean from the harbor that held a few hundred boats, the shark passed the harbor and headed toward the pillars of the pier. He ascended to swim close to the surface under the pier. His dorsal fin broke the surface of the water in the dim light as the first rays of the morning sun spilled up into the eastern sky but the light had not yet reached the gloomy darkness of the ocean. The mountains kept the sun from spreading its light to this murky domain of the shark. The ocean remained a shadowy unknown grave where the shark ruled in the dark.

Once past the pier the shark swam closer to the shore about thirty feet from the land. He again spotted some splashing in the water. A lone swimmer was moving along the surface of the water. The shark turned around toward the open sea and made a second pass near the swimmer. But the swimmer was now walking on the sand toward the shore. The shark could only see the white soles as the feet moved out of the water.

The shark again moved out toward the open sea. In front of him he spotted a school of fifty or more dolphins. But dolphins could be difficult prey. They were fast and in large groups they were aggressive. But this was not the prey he was looking for.

Past Montecito the shark moved closer to the shore where the first surfers of the day had started to gather. The boys were resting on their boards with their black wetsuit legs swinging back and forth in the ocean as the first rays of the early morning sun started spilling over the Santa Ynez Mountains. The land, sky and sea formed one unit of grayness in the early morning light. Stripes of oranges and gold in the eastern sky promised a beautiful day.

The shark kept its distance from the group of surfers. Swimming low against the floor of the ocean his white belly at times touched the sand and rock of the sea floor. The shark swam around in the small bay just north of Carpinteria and make a second pass near the surfers. His movements were slow and calculated. He watched the arms and legs of several of the surfers moving through the water, their white boards picking up all the light the sun gave so early in the day. Again the shark turned around in the small bay between Montecito and Carpenteria. The shark made a third pass. There was only the ocean. And man. And the shark. The shark swam back out into the great ocean.

CHAPTER 2

7:48 AM:

"Hey, I think I saw something out there," a young man nearly nineteen years old said to his buddy that morning.

"You're always seeing something" his friend replied not too interested in his remark. "It was probably just some stranglers from the school of dolphins that passed a few minutes ago."

"Yea, you're probably right," the boy replied but he kept his eyes peeled on the surface of the water about twenty feet from where he and his friend were sitting on their surfboards.

The sun was just making a break past the mountains. The day was sweet. The first rays of the sunlight were hot and suddenly warmed the coolness left by the summer night.

"Hey, it's Toad-man," the second boy said.

The first boy turned around toward the shore to see another surfer heading out with his board. The third surfer was already past walking on the sand and had slid his body onto the board as his arms reached down into the water. His strong arms pulled himself and his board out to join his friends.

As the third boy reached the other two, he said to them, "Any action yet?"

At that moment the first boy's leg was torn off his body as a massive mouth lined with teeth grabbed it. The shark's teeth were so sharp that the boy didn't feel them cut and tear off his leg, he only felt the enormous pressure of the three thousand pound fish that shook the boy's body. As the boy looked down at his leg now missing pass his knee, another shark ripped out of the water to clench the second boy's board and part of his thigh. As the first boy screamed out in agony, the third boy had fallen off his board by the force of a shark's swift body. He plunged down into the water, his head sideways with his arms and legs struggling in the water. He was eaten whole by an enormous white shark, leaving only a part of one his arms with the hand still attached floating in the water.

A task force of sharks attacked the twenty-four surfers gathered in the waters off Santa Barbara that day. A shark rushed a surfer as he made his way toward the shore. The gigantic creature seized the boy by this back, biting clear through so only the boy's head and legs remained in the water. Another shark quickly came behind and finished off the head and neck of the boy.

A shark zoomed in on another surfer lying on his board. He plucked the boy along with his board out of the water. The shark's vast mouth moved several times as he swallowed the boy leaving only his feet that floated in the bloody water.

In the frenzy of the assault a smaller shark was bitten by one of his comrades. In a moment his shredded body was also devoured.

One of the surfers had managed to avoid being bitten. He was nearly at the shore when he was rushed from behind. The strength of the shark's push knocked the boy down. The shark bit off one of the boy's legs before swimming back toward the deeper water.

Watching his friends being devoured, one of the teenagers ran to the land his feet stumbling in the sand and rocks. His arm was missing from the shoulder. As he fell to the beach the sharks left as quickly as they had appeared.

CHAPTER 3

7:50 AM:

Gloria Town was sitting at her breakfast table looking over the morning paper. Her children had left the house five minutes before along with her husband. Her house sat on a prime piece of land just south of the Biltmore Hotel in Montecito. Something caught her eye and she looked up from her paper to see the enfolding scene. Her mind reached around to comprehend the scene she was watching. As her heart raced, her head exploded in terror. She could see from her house the carnage below in the water.

It took her several moments before she could make herself walk toward the phone only a few feet away from her. Her hand trembled as she picked up the phone. Her mouth worked to find some words, but nothing came out. The fingers of her hands smashed the keys on her phone in no particular order.

"Shh . . . ark. Shark," she shouted into the dead phone.

Hearing nothing she fell to the floor moaning as her body dropped against the refrigerator door. Again her legs found their strength and she moved her body up the wall to again glance at the scene below. Turning around crying against the cold wall, her finger found the numbers 9 . . . 1 . . . 1.

"Hello, This is the 911 operator. Can I help you?" a woman's voice came over the phone.

"Shark, shark," Gloria yelled into the phone.

"Where are you, ma'am?"

"At my house. There is a . . . shark attack . . . on the beach . . . in front of my house," the woman coughed into the phone.

"A shark attack?"

"Yes, hundreds of sharks, they're attacking . . ." Gloria's voice fell off into sobs.

"Okay, ma'am, okay. Stay on the line. We're sending someone there right now. Just try to calm down. Remember stay on the line."

The operator hearing the woman's cries quickly called the Coast Guard. She waited for someone to answer the phone at the Coast Guard's office.

CHAPTER 4

7:56 AM:

Duncan Burton had just walked into his office. The phone was already ringing. He threw down his keys in disgust as his right hand reached to pick up the phone. It was rare to get a phone call so early in the morning although during the summer the office stayed busy from morning until sunset with a variety of problems—drunks driving boats, sometimes a stranded boat that ran out of gas. Just your regular coast guard stuff.

"United States Coast Guard," his voice was hoarse with the first words he had spoken that day.

"Hello, this is the 911 operator. We just got a call of a shark attack in progress."

"An attack, where?"

"A woman called from her house. Apparently she saw it from her house in Montecito. It's near the Biltmore. She's hysterical. Her house is on Sealane Shore."

"That's overlooking the point. That's where all the surfers go," Duncan knew the address because as a teenager he often surfed off that point that produced the best waves in the area.

"Yea, she says there's hundred of sharks," the operator relayed the information with doubt in her voice.

"Did she say how many people are involved?"

"No, I've still got her on the line but she unable to talk. She's hysterical."

"Thanks, I'll pick you on my phone in the truck."

Duncan picked up his keys and ran out the door. He imagined the sighting involved the school of dolphins that often swim along the Santa Barbara shore in the morning hours. But a report of a shark attack prompted him to react quickly to the spot. Certainly the waters off the coast of Santa Barbara were home to the Great White shark. They fed off the seals that congregate and bred on the Santa Barbara Channel Islands. As a matter of fact the waters off this part of the California coast were the deadliest waters in the world for Great White shark attacks.

There had been a few shark attacks in the past ten years.

A man was eaten in Avila bay near San Luis Obispo. A surfer was killed off the beach on Vandenberg Air Force Base. The last one involved a conch diver who had his leg bitten off just as he was getting on board his boat a mile or so off one of the Santa Barbara Islands. He died before a helicopter was able to get to him. A few years before that, two kyackers were missing a little south of Santa Barbara. The woman was found with a major part of her thigh and ass bitten off. The man was never found, but both kayaks were found and both had gigantic shark bites. The attack was definitely a Great White. The Great White rule these waters today as much as they had ruled them for the past million years. Even the original Indian tribe here, the Cushumas, had legends about the Great White shark. The shark had always meant death.

There is the triangle of ocean known as white death that is just north of Santa Barbara to San Francisco. This triangle of ocean water had more white shark attacks than anywhere in the world. And when a Great White attacks a human being the result is usually death.

As Duncan was walking to his car he saw one of his officers in the parking lot talking with a woman roller-skater.

"Tom," Duncan said not waiting for a reply, "We've got trouble. A shark attack down at the point. Leave a note in the office for Connie then follow me down in your car."

As Duncan got into his car he could hear the woman with Tom say, "A shark attack, cool."

CHAPTER 5

8:06 AM:

When Duncan arrived at the scene he could see two survivors lying on the beach. A woman runner was kneeling next to one of the boys with his head on her lap. Her pants were taken off and formed a bandage on the boy's leg that was missing from the knee down. The boy's blond hair was matted with his blood and sand. The woman stroked his head with her bloody hand as she held his bandaged leg with her other hand. He was in shock, his body rippling from the assault he had suffered a few minutes before.

About ten feet away another boy laid with his face in the sand. Or rather what was left of the boy's body. This torso had been bitten in half somewhere around the groin. He was obviously dead but an older man was pacing near the body yelling, "He's dying, he's dying."

Another dark haired boy was in a few inches of the water on his knees. The waves lapped against him as his head fell into the few inches of water. The boy's arm from the shoulder down was gone. As Duncan could see from where he stood on the top of the dune, another man was running out toward the fallen boy to help him out of the water.

What remained in the water were bits of surfboards and body parts in an ocean of red. Duncan ran back to his truck and called on his phone to the 911 operator.

"Hello, what's the problem?" the operator answered.

"This is Officer Burton from the Coast Guard. You just called me about a shark attack. It's bad. It looks like there are several fatalities. Call all the ambulances available and the call the sheriff. We're going to have to close the area."

Duncan looked back toward the Pacific Coast Highway. The traffic was already slowing down to look at the bloody sea.

"And call the Highway Patrol," he told the operator. "We may have some problems along the 101 for the looksy-loos. We're going to need all the help we can get."

"Were there a hundred sharks?" the operator asked.

"I don't know. I don't know what happened. But whatever it was, it's bad. It's very bad."

As Duncan ran down to the beach he approached the woman who was comforting the wounded boy as she seemed the most reliable witness because she was the only one was somewhat calm.

"What happened?" Duncan asked her.

"I was running on the beach when I saw the sharks come. There were so many of them," she said as her voice trembled betraying her fear despite the fact her face looked calm.

"How many surfers were out there?" Duncan asked.

"I don't know . . . maybe twenty or thirty."

The older man who was standing over the dead boy ran over to Duncan as he screamed, "They came like an army. They killed them all. Look at them," he wandered off as he continued raving. "Do you have a gun? You have to kill them? Do you hear me? Kill them, you have to kill them. They didn't have any fear . . . those sharks . . . they just . . ."

"All right, sir, all right sir, just calm down. Please get a hold of yourself. We're going to need your report," Duncan told the man.

The words seemed to help the man get a hold of his senses for a moment. He fell down and wept near the dead boy's body.

"Did you notice the sharks before the attack," Duncan again questioned the woman.

"No, there was nothing. Not even a ripple of water. It was so beautiful here. And so quiet. It was so calm and peaceful here just a moment before."

Duncan knelt down near the boy body's and looked at the bandage the woman had made around the boy's leg. It seemed good enough for now. The leg was only bleeding a little and Duncan tighten the bandage.

God, I hope the ambulances get here soon. I don't want this boy bleeding to death, Duncan thought. He made his mind again focus on questioning the woman.

"And then you noticed the sharks when they . . . when they began to attack the surfers?" he asked her.

"Yes. It was like an ambush. Something calculated and quickly executed. Everything happened so quickly. And then they were gone as quickly as the came."

"How long would you say it lasted?"

"Not more than five minutes."

All these boys dead in less than five minutes, Duncan thought to himself in disbelief. It had to be more than one shark.

"Did you notice how many sharks were involved," he asked the woman.

"I don't know, but there were lots of them."

"Maybe three or four," Duncan wanted the estimate to be low so the woman wouldn't be prompted to exaggerate. But even Duncan knew three or four White sharks could not kill about twenty men in less than five minutes.

"I don't know. Maybe fifteen or twenty."

Tom pulled up in his jeep. He ran down the beach to find Duncan with the woman.

"My God, what's happened?" Tom asked Duncan as he walked up to him.

Bits of left over human body parts were beginning to drift to the shore. Duncan looked down at what appeared to be intestines lying on the beach like seaweed.

"We've had several fatalities. Apparently there were several sharks who . . . attack the group of surfers who normally come here in the morning."

"Where is everybody?" Tom asked at his surveyed the nearly empty beach.

"I think . . . I think most of them are dead. This lady says she saw about twenty surfers out in the ocean before the attack."

"That can't be," Tom replied in disbelief.

"Listen, Tom, I already called the ambulances and the sheriff. Stay here and try to keep out anyone not authorized from entering the beach until the police come. When the ambulances get here send them to that boy first . . . I think he's in shock. Then the other boy . . . the one without an arm. That one's dead," he motioned his head to the boy lying dead in the surf.

"Should I at least pull him all the way out of the water," Tom asked about the corpse.

"Yes, but don't take long. I'm going to check on that boy over there . . . the one without an arm. I need to put something on his arm to stop the bleeding until the ambulances get here. You got to keep people out of here until the police come."

CHAPTER 6

8:32 AM:

Ten minutes later Duncan had some help. The ambulances were just taking the two survivors to the hospital. The remaining body parts of the surfers were coming up regularly now to the shore pushed in by the early tide. The police had taped off the area and were now assisting in the recovery of the remains. Duncan's other officers had been called and where now arriving in their boats to form a safety barrier between the site and the open sea.

Sergeant Dick Harry from the Santa Barbara Police Department walked up to Duncan.

"Do they think the boys will survive?" Duncan asked him.

"Yes, yea. They took Mr. Cannel with them too."

"Mr. Cannel?" Duncan questioned the Sergeant.

"Yea, the man who was going crazy. They put him under sedation."

"But I need to talk with him. He's a witness."

"He's not going to do you any good. The man's gone bonkers."

Duncan looked down in disgust at the Sergeant's remark.

"What's all those boats doing out there?" the Sergeant questioned Duncan.

"We're setting up a perimeter so we can recover the . . . bodies remaining in the water."

"You're going into the ocean . . . with all that blood. What about the sharks?"

"We've got to go in. We've got to recover . . . what's left of the bodies. And we think the sharks are all gone. I haven't spotted one since I've been here."

"Who can spot a shark under the surface of the water. I think you're a crazy man sending people down in the ocean with all that blood in the water. Even if the attacking sharks are gone, there bound to be others picking up what's left. Sharks can smell blood from miles away, can't they? You'll soon have every shark and his brother here. It's just one great big feeding ground to them now."

"I've got to get those bodies out of the water. That's the only evidence we have," Duncan said determined to do the impossible.

"Evidence? What do you need evidence for? Are you planning on taking the offending sharks to court?" the Sergeant said with a laugh.

Duncan did not appreciate the Sergeant's wry comment.

"We don't know what really happened here. Or how many victims there were . . . but we've got to do what we can to figure it out. And we've got to pick the remaining bodies."

"Well, I know I'm not going in there. And none of my men are," the Sergeant said.

"No, I don't expect you to. Just keep the beach free and gather what evidence comes to the shore. I've got some divers coming. And we're putting them in shark cages for safety. I assure you, Sergeant, I intend to lose no more men to sharks."

The Sergeant's back was to the sea as he was looking at the Pacific Coast Highway running by the ocean.

"It looks like the CHP have there hands full too because of this. Look at all the cars already on the Pacific Coast Highway."

"Hum," Duncan said as he turned his face to look at the highway. Hundreds of cars were backed up and driving slowly to look at the site as the Highway Patrolmen tried to keep the traffic moving. "The looksey loos are already out," Duncan said. "By tomorrow, this town will be full of looksey loos. They will all want to see the sharks. They'll expect to see them swimming in some school like the dolphins do off the coast."

"Yep, and I have to say there's a lot to look at today. It's going to be a very interesting day for all of us," the Sergeant said before he walked away looking at some unidentifiable body part as he walked back up to the road.

"Hey, don't forget this thing," the Sergeant yelled to one of his men. "It's . . . hell, I don't know what it is, but it looks like its some part of the human body."

CHAPTER 7

8:52 AM:

The first reporter from the Santa Barbara Newspaper arrived with his photographer in tow. Five minutes later the local television stations were setting up their positions to film the recovering operation. Several of the local news morning anchors were positioned on the bluff overlooking the sea giving their viewers the first look of the attack.

"Santa Barbara attacked," said one of the woman reporters into the camera . . . "a vicious pack of great white sharks attacked several surfers off the coast this morning. There are multiple deaths, the only question is—how many? Stay tuned for upcoming news as we will be bringing you the latest updates on this terrifying attack."

As Duncan walked up to his car to call the town's mayor, he heard another reporter say, "But what can you expect when you're surfing in the shark's backyard."

Duncan flinched at the comment but made his way to his truck to call the mayor to inform him of the seriousness of the problem. Some of the reporters left there post to follow him to his car.

"Can you tell us how many are dead?" one of them asked.

"What are you going to do to protect the people of Santa Barbara from further attacks?" another one asked.

Duncan slammed the door to his truck shut so he could have a little privacy. What am I going to do to protect the people here, he thought. How can you protect a population that insists on going in the ocean when sharks swim freely around. And how can you prevent a shark from doing what's its been doing for millions of years.

"I'm afraid Santa Barbara will be all over the news today," Duncan told the stunned mayor. "We know there are two survivors and one confirmed dead, but there are a lot of bodies floating out in the water."

By 9:14 the helicopters started arriving sweeping low over the ocean as the Coast Guard boats started launching the first shark cages with the divers into the water. The eight Coast Guard boats from Santa Barbara and Ventura sat in the water off the coast forming a sort of barrier between the coastal waters and the open sea. The Coast Guard boats from Los Angeles had been sent up as backup to keep the curious boaters away from the area. They were now just arriving on the scene.

"You've got to get those guys out of here," Duncan yelled at Sergeant Harry as he pointed to the helicopters flying close to his boats.

"Can't do that. It's free space," the Sergeant yelled back over the noise of the helicopters.

"Then at least tell them to keep their distance, they're causing waves in the water. It's going to be hard enough for the divers without the helicopters stirring up the water."

By 9:45, the reporters from Los Angeles started arriving. The coverage was continuous with cameras and reporters stationed wherever they could find a spot. More than twenty different stations had sent crews to pick up the story. Even the major national networks had television crews there to film the rescue operations.

Duncan went out on one of the motorboats to view the first remains picked up by the divers. A sachet of body parts in a net was thrown on the deck. Duncan saw what was clearly a hand and part of a head in the mess of white tissue and bloody remains. He turned away in disgust as he said to his lead diver.

"Don't open the bags on the decks. Take them below until can take them to the corridor's office for examination. Showing the guts like this will turn that mob of reporters into sharks themselves."

CHAPTER 8

11:36 AM:

By late morning Duncan was able to return to his office. Outside the Coast Guard building was a pack of reporters pushing microphones into his face and stumbling along with him as he walked. The reporters asked him questions as he tried to out run them to his office door.

"What happened?" one of the reporters asked shoving the microphone into Duncan's face.

"Can you tell us how many people where killed?" another report asked.

"Were any sharks killed?" still another reporter asked in quick succession.

Duncan frowned at the last question as though there was any way a 170-pound man could kill a 2,000 or 3,000 pound shark with his bare hands.

"I have no comment at this time," Duncan replied as he tried to open the door to the office. It was locked. He pulled out his keys when he was smashed against the door by the wave of people pressing toward him. With an effort he opened the door, then shut the door behind him.

He leaned against the door.

"Shit," he said.

"Duncan, thank God you're back," Connie, the secretary at the office, said. "It's been a mess, an absolute mess here today. There's

18

been calls all morning. I finally had to lock the door because everyone keeps coming in asking all sorts of questions about what happened. What did happen?"

"I don't think you really want to know," Duncan said as he threw his keys on his desk.

"I do. Tell me," she said rising out of her chair to perch herself on top of the corner of her desk to listen to Duncan.

"There were a group of about twenty surfers at the point," Duncan started talking with a monotone voice, "and a group of sharks . . ."

"A group, I thought sharks only traveled solo," Connie asked curiously.

"Yes, that's usually true. But according to the witnesses a group of sharks came and attacked the surfers simultaneously."

"How many did they kill?"

"I don't know exactly, but most of the surfers there this morning, I think. There were only three survivors. I mean two. One of the boys died on the beach."

"Oh, my God," Connie grimaced at the thought. At that moment frantic knocking was heard at the door.

"Not another one. Just ignore it, they'll go away," Connie said waving her hand in the air.

The knocking continued. Then a woman's voice was heard.

"Hello, Officer Burton, this is Lt. Reynolds from the United States Navy."

Duncan and Connie looked at each other neither knowing how to respond.

"Hello, hello, I know you've in there. This is Lt. Reynolds from the United States Navy, let me in," the woman's voice demanded.

Duncan walked over the door and crack it opened so that only his head could peak out. There was a woman, about twenty-five years old, her dark hair pinned up tight against her head with a white officer's cap perched on top. Her uniform was sparkling white. She did not smile but looked seriously at Duncan almost as if she were angry at him.

"Officer Burton?" she asked in a crisp manner.

"Yes," he replied.

The crowd of reporters surged around the door when they saw him at the door. Again came the questions from the reporters, "Can you tell us anything . . . how many dead are there?"

"Quick, come in," Duncan instructed the woman as he opened the door wider to let her in. The woman pushed in as the crowd of reporters gathered closer to her.

Duncan slammed the door shut as he closed his eyes simultaneously once the woman was inside.

"Hello, I'm Lt. Reynolds," the woman said holding out her hand.

Duncan opened his eyes and looked at the woman standing before him and her manicured nails trimmed short. He looked down at his own hand dirty with blood and sand. He wiped his hand on his blood smeared uniform, which only a few hours before had been as white as the woman's uniform.

They shook hands as the woman looked down at his dirty clothes. She then looked at Connie with an air of superiority. "Can we speak, in private?" she said with a glance toward Connie.

"Ah, sure," Duncan said with some hesitancy as to what he should do. "Connie, can you run over to the grill and get me something to eat. Would you like anything, Lt . . ."

". . . Reynolds. No, thank you," she replied.

Connie left the office obviously perturbed at being asked to leave and missing out on the conversation. Duncan and the woman walked into his office.

"You've been to the site already?" she asked.

"Yes, yes. I just came back."

"Is everything under control?"

The stress of the morning had almost made Duncan giddy. He wondered how you could ever control great white sharks.

"I . . . I guess," he answered her.

"Can you brief me?" she asked with concern in her voice about his capability.

"Yes, who are you?" he asked irritated at her interrogation of him. The last thing he needed after this morning was some woman asking him questions.

"I'm Lt. Reynolds from the United States Navy," she replied.

"So, you've told me. But why are you here?"

"I'm part of the Navy's team of shark specialists," she answered.

"Shark specialist? The Navy has a team of shark specialist?" Duncan asked. He already knew the Navy had a special group dedicated to shark research, but he fayed his ignorance.

"Yes. After the U.S. Indiana incident . . ." she explained.

"The U.S. Indiana incident? What are you talking about?" he asked her.

"During World War II, one of our ships went down in the Pacific," the woman began to explain. "It was the ship that carried the bombs that were later used in Japan. Anyway, the ship was torpedoed and went down. Because of the sensitive nature of the ship's mission, rescue ships were not immediately sent out. A thousand men went into the ocean. When the rescue boats did arrive four days later, there were less than 200 survivors. We lost over 800 men in four days because of . . . because of sharks. They systematically came and . . . fed off the men in the water. The survivors from the downed ship became a feeding ground for the sharks. Since that time the Navy has conducted research into shark behavior. I am part of that team."

"And you're here because . . ."

"The Navy scans all the news. When it became apparent that this was no single shark attack, that it was a group of sharks, I was sent to investigate."

"Where are you from?" he asked.

"Washington."

"DC?"

"Yes."

"You flew out here this morning."

"Yes, I got the call at 8:43 this morning," she said briskly.

Duncan looked at this watch. It was now 11:52.

"That was only four hours ago. How did you get here so fast?" he asked in amazement.

"The United States Navy is capable of many things," she said smiling. It was the first time he had seen her smile. She was kind of pretty, he thought, in an official sort of way. If she wasn't in that suit and had her hair pinned back so tightly, he might even consider her fair game.

"Obviously. And so what do you plan on doing here?" he asked her.

"I plan on finding out exactly what happened and report back to Washington."

"I don't know if I can help you."

"You are responsible here, are you not? Or should I be talking to someone else?" she replied as her eyes narrowed.

"Yes, I'm in charge here."

The woman again smiled as she looked him over. But it was not a kind smile but one of superiority as though she doubted he was capable of . . . much.

Duncan was aware that he was being summed up. He was a bachelor at thirty-two. He had been married once when he was twenty-five, but that didn't last long. His dark hair was wavy and cut short. His brown eyes flickered with interest. He watched as the woman's eyes traveled down his body to his feet. He sat on the side of his desk so he could escape her wandering eyes.

"I was the first one on the scene," Duncan could hear himself defending himself, "but . . . I still don't know what happened. Shit, I don't even now how many boys are dead."

Now, even he doubted his capability.

"We're there many?" she asked.

"Yes, I think about twenty people are dead. The police are handling calls about missing persons, specially those known to surf. But we don't even have any bodies."

"No. You wouldn't. Can we go out to the site?"

"There's nothing to see there now. I have divers in shark cages in the area picking up . . . the bodies or what's left of them."

"Still, I need to go."

"But what can we do? Even when we know how many dead there are? What do we do then?" Duncan asked.

"We make sure it doesn't happen again," she replied.

"And how can we do that. There's a whole ocean out there. What if these sharks start to like eating humans? What if they start hitting every beach along the California coast at dinner time."

"That's why I'm here. If this behavior is new, if it's part of the evolution of sharks . . . that they now hunt in packs and more specifically that they hunt humans, the government will act."

"What do you mean act?"

"The United States government is not about to let its population be threatened in any way. By anyone. Or by anything."

"What do you mean?" Duncan asked horrified at the woman's implications. "Do you mean the United States Government means to kill all the sharks off the California coast."

"Of course not, but . . ."

"But what?"

"But let's not jump the gun before we get started. Let's assimilate what really happened here today and why."

Just as Duncan and Lt. Reynolds were about to walk out the door Connie returns with the sandwich.

"You're leaving?" Connie asked as she opened the door to find Duncan with his keys in his hand.

"Yea, I'm taking Lt. Reynolds to the site," Duncan said embarrassed that he had forgotten he had sent Connie to get him something to eat.

"What about your lunch?" Connie asked annoyed with her boss.

Duncan looked at the sandwich. He was starving. He then looked at Lt. Reynolds.

"I'll eat later," Duncan said taking the sandwich with him as he walked out the door with Lt. Reynolds.

CHAPTER 9

1:43 P.M.

As Lt. Reynolds suggested, Duncan took her down to the beach near Montecito where only six hours before the shark attack had occurred. After reviewing the site, which was still manned by the police department as they tried to keep the hundreds of people who had gathered to look at the site off the beach, Duncan and Lt. Reynolds went out to the one of the boats to view what had been picked up. Most everything that could be recovered in the moving ocean had been recovered. Even the red seawater of the morning was gone, swept away by the waves and the currents. Mother nature had cleaned up the area efficiently and quickly. Two coast guard boats were stationed in the area looking for further evidence. There were no further sightings of sharks in the area. The other remaining boats where now helping the Coast Guard from Ventura keep the boaters away from the marked off area.

Afterwards, Duncan and Lt. Reynolds went to the morgue to view the body parts that had been collected in the morning. The coroner was taking the fingerprints from one of the hands that had no body or name attached to it as Duncan and Lt. Reynolds entered the room.

"Have you any idea how many people were killed out there today?" Lt. Reynolds asked the coroner as he rubbed the body less hand with ink.

"It looks like twenty-two," he said without any hesitation.

After Lt. Reynolds inspected a few of the body parts for evidence of the size of the sharks, she said to Duncan.

"It's definitely a great white, or I should say several great whites. And they're big ones too. Look at the size of this tooth," she said as she showed Duncan one of the shark's tooth that remained in the thigh of one of the legs. She plucked out the shark's tooth that was stuck in the bloody tissue.

It took every bit of strength for Duncan to stay in that room with her. The smell of dead human flesh rose through his nose to every fiber of his being. He was now glad he didn't have time to eat anything today.

Finally, at 5:30, Lt. Reynolds was finished looking through the evidence. Lt. Reynolds and Duncan walked out into the bright sun of a summer day in Santa Barbara. The day was hot, but where they stood was cool under some Sycamore trees. Duncan was happy to be outside, in the fresh air, and he walked with Lt. Reynolds over to Alameda Park.

"I need to see the survivors," Angie said, not noticing the beauty of the day as her face was bent down to the concrete that they walked on.

"They're at Cottage Hospital. I'll take you," Duncan replied. They hopped in his car for the five-minute drive to Cottage Hospital.

The doctor, who had stitched up the boy with the missing arm, was still on duty.

"He will survive," Lt. Reynolds stated more as an expectation than a question when she spoke to the doctor.

"Yes, of course," the doctor replied. "He did suffer massive blood loss. And he was, of course, in shock. But he's stable now. But we have him under sedation."

"Still, I'd like to look at him," she replied.

The doctor looked at her with disapproval. Lt. Reynolds looked back at him with determination.

"We are running an investigation here," she said. "I need to see the boy."

"Yes, okay," the doctor consented.

"And the other boy?" she asked. "What about him?"

"I expect he will survive too. We were lucky to get to him quickly. He suffered major blood loss . . . but I think he will pull through. We have him in intensive care."

"Fine, if I can see them now," Lt. Reynolds asserted.

"They both under sedation. You can't question them in any case," the doctor replied.

Lt. Reynolds simply smiled at the doctor.

"No, I wouldn't expect to question them now. But still I'd like to see them."

They visited the armless boy first. Inside the small room he laid on the bed, his shoulder bandaged. The area where his arm should have been was empty. She only stayed a minute before she asked to see the other boy.

The doctor along Lt. Reynold and Duncan again went into a small room, where in a single bed a boy without a leg was sleeping. The room was quiet except for the sound of the machine that was breathing for the boy. The Lt. looked at the boy, but her face remained hard and without expression.

Duncan looked away from the boy because he saw himself lying there. Those boys who had died at the beach that morning were like him—they simply loved to surf. That was their crime—that they like to surf. Because of that, they had died.

When they left the room, Duncan looked at Lt. Reynolds's face. Her face was pale, but devoid of emotion. He drove her back to his office. A few reporters still hung around as Duncan and Lt. Reynolds quickly went inside. It was now 7:00, and the sun was starting its slow descent into the western sky leaving Santa Barbara in a red glow. They were alone as Connie had left the office several hours ago.

"Want some coffee? Or anything?" he asked her.

"No," she answered automatically.

He again looked at her face. She was concentrating hard as she wrote in her little book. Everything about her annoyed him. She didn't seem to care about anything or anybody. These boys were just corpses to her. But to Duncan, they were himself. It could have been him who was in the water ten years ago. It could have been him who was lying on that table, just a hand without a body. Just a body without a name.

"Doesn't any of this bother you?" he finally asked her.

She looked up at him surprised by his question.

"It's just business," she said looking back down at her notes.

"Ah, just business. There are twenty-two dead boys and it's just business," he said.

Her eyebrows closed in together as she looked at him.

"I plan on going to San Francisco tomorrow," she said as if their conversation of the past few minutes had not taken place.

"San Francisco, why?" he asked.

"To visit, Lucky DeSanto," she answered matter of factly.

"Who's he?" Duncan asked.

"He is the foremost great white shark expert in the world. He operates the Great White Shark Research Institute off the coast just above San Francisco. It's the bloody triangle. We often use him as an expert with our great white studies. Want to come along?" she asked Duncan as one corner of her mouth lifted up in expectation.

"I wouldn't miss it for the world," Duncan replied.

CHAPTER 10

7:34 **AM**:

The next morning Duncan and Lt. Reynolds flew to the San Francisco airport. On the plane, Lt. Reynolds reviewed with Duncan Lucky DeSanto's background.

"Lucky is a great white survivor. When he was twenty-two years old he was surfing in South Africa . . ."

"Is he South African?" Duncan asked.

"No, he's Australian. But he was a beach bum when he was younger. He did all the great surfing beaches . . . Australia, South Africa, Hawaii, California. He just traveled around from place to place surfing."

"And he was actually attacked by a great white?"

"Yes. It was late in the day and he was taking just one more run when a great white came and bit his surfboard. Lucky was knocked off into the water. The shark then came back and bit Lucky in his ribs. But the shark let go. He had about two hundred stitches."

"So how do you think he's going to feel about the twenty-two surfers killed yesterday?" Duncan asked her.

"I don't know. He's traditionally a activist for the great white . . ."

"Even though he was bitten by one?"

"Well, as he says you don't get rid of cars just because you've been in an accident. He loves the ocean and I think it can be said that he even admires the great white shark for their beauty of their design."

"He sounds like quite a character," Duncan remarked.

"He is," she confirmed.

Lt. Reynolds was looking out at the ocean as they flew north over the California coast. She seemed lost in her thoughts as Duncan watched her.

"Can I call you something other than Lt. Reynolds . . . I mean that takes so long to say and since we're working together . . ." Duncan finally got up the nerve to ask her.

"Angie," she replied.

"Angie?"

"Yea, you can call me Angie," she said as a smile lit up her face.

"Oh, okay, Angie, I'm Duncan," he said making some attempt to get to know this woman in her white starched uniform.

"I know," she said again looking out over the Pacific Ocean as they flew north. "I actually know quite a lot about you. I read up on you on my flight out here."

"You read up on me?" Duncan asked amazed that there would be anything to read up on.

"Yes, I know you were born in Santa Barbara. That you went to the University of Santa Barbara and that you have a degree in Marine Biology. And that you were hired by the Coast Guard straight out of college."

"Is that all?" he asked curious to know what else she might know about him.

"No. I also know you were once married, but that you're divorce now," she said with a quick look to see what his expression would be.

"Oh, you do. And does that report tell you who I sleep with?" he asked almost angry at the fact that she had so much information about him, but he knew nothing about her.

Angie laughed.

"I'm afraid it doesn't go into that much detail."

"Thank God," Duncan said with a grimace. He did not like the fact that Angie knew so much about him, but he hardly even knew her first name.

At the airport they rented a car and drove north to Marin County. Lucky DeSanto had set up his research center on the coast where he could overlook the ocean and the mouth of San Francisco Bay. This was prime shark country. His research center was nothing more than a slab building sitting in the middle of a stark, treeless mountain.

The morning was fogged in as it usually was in the summer months. The view was nothing but a sea of fog. Angie parked the car in what looked like just an open field. Duncan followed Angie, as she seemed to know the way to the where they were going although he could see nothing as he walked into the fog.

"It's bleak here," Duncan said.

Angie ignored his comment as she quickly walked up to the door that appeared out of nowhere.

A man in his late forties answered the door. His hair was blond quickly turning gray and was long and hanging loosely around his face. The man's face was well tanned and unshaved. Years in the sun had formed crevices into his face. If Duncan were to see the man on the street, he would have taken him for a bum.

"Angie, I thought it was you," the man said as he opened the door as they were still walking down the dirt path toward him.

"Well, we've got a big problem, Lucky," she said to him as she shook his hand.

"So I hear on the news. Twenty-two dead. Two maimed survivors. That's a lot."

"Yea, what do you think," Angie asked Lucky forgetting about Duncan.

"Who's the boy scout?" Lucky asked viewing Duncan with some amusement.

"Oh, this is Duncan Burton. He's from the Santa Barbara Coast Guard. It's his jurisdiction."

"So you have a bunch of rogue sharks on your hands," Lucky said to Duncan.

Duncan could have been offended by Lucky's attitude, but he had known too many old surfers to take offense. That was just their talk. They made fun of everyone who was in a suit. Left over radicals from the Vietnam War days.

"Yea," was all Duncan managed to respond.

The man opened the door to let Angie and Duncan enter the small building. The walls were covered with hundreds of pictures of great white sharks—both alive and dead. There were pictures of sharks in the ocean eating from a large hunk of meat. The sharks massive mouth opened to reveal an endless pit of darkness. Other pictures showed great whites after they had been captured. They were oversized monsters that dwarfed the men who caught them. Duncan noticed in one of the pictures that the shark's tooth was as big as a man's hand.

The room was simply furnished but every surface was covered with magazines, papers, old food and dried up coffee cups. The room only had a desk, a couple of chairs, a television set, a refrigerator and small microwave. Lucky sat down on the one metal chairs. He remained quiet for a few moments as his mouth made strange movements like he was exaggerating the chewing of gum. But Angie wasn't about to leave him to his silence.

"So, Lucky, tell me, what do you think?" Angie asked.

"I don't know, Angie. I can't say I'm totally surprised. My research has found that great whites do probably hunt in packs. Of course, when I was young we thought they were loners. But since we've started tagging them, we find different sharks coming into one feed."

"Do you think this attack is some evolutional change or just some freak occurrence?"

"I don't know," Lucky replied. "Sharks are a key component in the ecology of the sea. If you mess around with some components, it's going to have an effect on something else. The great white is, of course, protected now. But other sharks aren't. They are still being fished at unprecedented numbers. And these are the sharks that are often the food of the great whites. If there are less of other sharks in the ocean, the great white is going to be forced to look somewhere else. If their traditional food no longer exists, it only makes sense that the sharks find a new food source. They have to, in order to survive."

Lucky was quiet for a moment as though he were considering the matter when Duncan asked him, "I hear you were attacked once by a great white?"

"Yea, the bastard bit me but good. Want to see the scars," Lucky offered as he got up from his chair and began to pull his shirt off before Duncan had a chance to reply.

"Sure," Duncan answered as Lucky lifted his arm to show the outline of scars which crossed his back and rib area. The bite print left from the sharks jaws where still clearly visible almost thirty years after the attack. Duncan inspected the area and flinched at the thought of his body in the jaws of the monster.

"The shark didn't bite threw?" Duncan asked.

"Naw, I wouldn't be here talking to you today if he had. He was just taking a little nibble to see if I was any good. But sharks, in general, don't prefer humans as food. We don't have enough fat on us. They prefer a nice, fat seal or walrus, something they can really sink their teeth into. I was probably just to damn skinny to bother with."

"Lucky," Angie interrupted, "I think this might be a new pattern."

"You do?" Lucky was baiting her even though he agreed with her.

"In the research I've done off some islands in the South Pacific, I noted that families of sharks live and feed off a single island. The larger female shark fed off one side of the island, while on the other side of the island a group of younger and smaller sharks fed. We consistently spotted the same group of sharks feeding in the same areas. They seemed to return to the same area every two weeks to ten days. It's like they had a little route they followed. By our estimation, they are her offspring. We did some DNA tests to confirm that they were. When we baited them with food, the smaller sharks always came in groups."

"And the dad?" Lucky asked. "Where was he?"

"We never spotted any larger male species. We figure he must be off in the open ocean somewhere."

"Yea . . ." Lucky replied.

Lucky remained quiet for a few moments as his mouth again made strange movements like he was exaggerating the chewing of gum.

"What is it?" Angie queried him.

"Just some thoughts I've had lately. It always made me think why we were only tagging smaller sharks off the coast here."

"Smaller sharks?" Duncan asked.

"Well, smaller in Great White terms. The largest shark we ever tagged was twenty, maybe twenty one feet long."

"That's sounds pretty big to me," Duncan said.

"Yea, the shark that got me was maybe twelve or thirteen feet, but he seemed pretty big to me at the time. But we've gotten reports of really big sharks . . . maybe thirty or more feet."

"Oh, my God," Duncan replied.

"And the thing about sharks is that as they get longer, they also increase their width."

"Their width?" Duncan asked.

"Yea, and that makes their weight increase. A fifteen footer might be 2,000 pounds. A twenty footer might be 3,000 pounds. Who knows how big those really big sharks might be out in the open ocean. But I wouldn't be surprised if there are some 5,000 pounds sharks swimming out there right now. Anyway, I've always wondered why we were only tagging smaller sharks less than twenty feet . . . and I've got a theory."

"What is it?" Angie asked.

"I think the larger male sharks stay in the open water. I think the sharks we see off the coasts are the smaller teenagers or females. The real kings are out there in the open ocean. It's too tough of a place for even the teenagers to survive. When they get big, they go out there to hunt," Lucky said pointing to the endless ocean, "where the real action is."

"What if those larger sharks came back to the coast to feed?" Angie asked.

"Yea, what if?" Lucky concurred.

"Do you think they're capable of hunting in groups?" Angie asked him.

"It's never been documented. But just because we don't know about it doesn't mean it doesn't exist."

"I think it's just been documented yesterday in Santa Barbara," Duncan replied.

Lucky nodded.

"What does your research say about group hunting?" Lucky asked Angie.

"We have some speculation," she confirmed.

"Oh?" Lucky said.

"Yes, with the beached whales. For years, we've done research as to why these groups of whales, sometimes hundreds of them, would beach themselves. It has been suggested that the whales have been chased and herded into bays for easy picking by sharks. That they whales are trying to get away from these sharks and they accidentally beach themselves."

"Because the alternative . . . to stay in the water . . . would be deadly even for a whale?" Lucky questioned her.

Angie nodded in reply.

"And this herding could only be accomplished by a pack of sharks?" Duncan asked.

"Yes, well, I don't see how one shark could cause so much terror that an entire colony of whales would face suicide rather than stay in the water and face what . . . what was out there," she said.

"Could that be possible?" Duncan replied at the thought.

"And the only shark really capable of that would be . . ." Angie continued.

". . . Would be the great white," Duncan finished her sentence.

"Perhaps," Lucky took up the thought. "But still you have not direct research confirming this, do you?"

"No, it's just a theory," she said.

"Well, it's on theories that life is finally understood," Lucky replied.

"So, do you find that totally unbelievable?" Angie questioned Lucky.

"No, no, not at all. I just heard last month about a swimmer in Australia who was bitten three different times within a few minutes. He thought it was the same shark. But when they measured the teeth marks, they found the shark bites were all different sizes leading me to believe . . ."

". . . It was three different sharks," Angie finished his sentence, "coming in to the same feeding."

"Exactly," Lucky replied.

"It sounds like we have ourselves some pack animals. And they're hungry," Duncan said.

At that moment Lucky, whose eyes were always scanning the ocean, said, "Looks like we've got some hungry sharks now."

As he reached for his binoculars, Angie and Duncan both looked out of the windows to see the ocean below. In the few minutes since their arrival, the fog had pushed out farther out in the ocean and formed a wall of mist on the western horizon. Duncan and Angie spotted below in the ocean a tiny eruption of water. To most observers, it would appear as nothing.

"Yep, we've got a feeding. Looks like a bull got it today," Lucky confirmed.

"Let me see," Angie said taking the binoculars from Lucky.

"Want to go down and see?" Lucky asked Duncan.

"Sure," Duncan said hesitantly a little after hearing about 5,000 pounds monsters of the ocean only a few minutes earlier.

"I need to call Stog," Lucky said before he picked up the phone and dialed a number.

"Stog?" Duncan questioned Angie as to what a "Stog" referred to since he thought it might be some office acronym.

"Stog is his photographer. He lives in the house over there."

Duncan looked out the back window to see another house that had just been hidden a few minutes before by the fog.

"Stog, we got one going," Duncan heard Lucky say into the phone. "Okay, he's coming, let's go," Lucky said as he started herding them outside and into the jeep.

Lucky started up the jeep and drove by the other house where a man appeared. He came running out of the house, his heavy belly pushing his T-shirt up to expose belly-button. His stomach rippled with fat as he ran to the car. He jumped in the back seat next to Duncan, but didn't say a word to Duncan or even acknowledge his presence.

"So, maybe we'll get some good ones today," Stog said before covering his nose with both of his hands and blowing into them. Whatever was deposited into his hands from his nose was quickly wiped off on his pants.

CHAPTER 11

11:23 AM:

Lucky drove the jeep down on narrow and steep dirt road to a small dock on the ocean. Tied up to the makeshift dock was a 14-foot motorboat. Duncan followed the frenzy as everyone ran to the boat. They were going out to sea. Stog went immediately below as Lucky started up the engine.

"Where's he going?" Duncan asked Angie as Lucky steered the boat toward the small splashing they had seen from the top of the mountain.

"He's loading some film in his camera," Angie told him.

"You've done this before with them?" Duncan asked her.

"Yea, I've spent quite a bit of time with both of these guys," she said as her eyes searched the surface of the ocean for signs of the feeding that was taking place.

Duncan again looked at the woman who had come into this life just yesterday morning. She had removed her hat. When Stog came out from cabin, Angie went below. She came out three minutes later. Her uniform was off and instead she wore a pair of dungarees and a t-shirt with the University of Central Florida emblazed on it. Duncan had never noticed her breasts before but now he did. Her hair was down from its bun and she was pulling it back in a ponytail with her arms raised above her head. Angie noticed Duncan looking at her and gave him a knowing smile in her eyes in return.

"Yep, here we are kids . . . it's Seymour time," Lucky said as the boat approached the commotion in the water.

"Seymour time, what's that?" Duncan said.

"Oh, that's Lucky's name for The Shark. He's made up a little song that he always sings," she said. Then she began to sing the song, "It's Seymour, the friendly white shark . . ."

Lucky and Stog joined her for the rest of the song that was sung like a child's tune,

". . . It's Seymour, the friendly white shark.

It's Seymour, the friendly white shark.

He'll either smile at you or eat you up . . . eat you up . . .

eat you up."

Duncan wondered at the strange company he was keeping in the middle of the ocean on a 14-foot boat with 5,000 pounds sharks swimming around. He wished he were home watching Baywatch reruns or a Laker's game.

The boat stopped at the remains of a large bull. His 4,000 pounds of blubber and fat had been reduced to a few bits of flesh left in the water. As Stog started taking pictures, Lucky yelled, "Ohh, ohh baby, go, go, go."

Everyone in the boat watch the sharks attack the corpse of the bull as Lucky steered the boat near the action. A shark slashed through the depths of the water to grab a piece of the flesh with its pointed teeth. Duncan had never seen a great white before in person and froze back in fear as he watched the prehistorically designed animal devour its prey. With the ease of a knife through soft butter, the shark ripped off an extended piece of the flesh. Duncan could only see one shark. But in another second, another shark came into the kill and tore another piece of soft tissue from the dead animal. Again and again the sharks came to finish off their meal with vigor. Duncan was amazed at the size of the mammoth creatures when Lucky said, "See what I mean, Angie, little babies. These guys are only sixteen or so feet. Not much bigger than this boat."

The observation did not comfort Duncan. Lucky was right. He may be complaining that these were the little Great White sharks but these sharks were bigger than the boat on which these four human lives depended on.

"Do they ever attack boats?" Duncan felt compelled to ask before he would urge them back to shore.

"What's wrong, boy," Lucky callously asked him, "Scared?"

"They rarely attack boats," Angie replied in a military like manner.

"Yes, well, up to yesterday, they rarely attacked groups of surfers killing . . ." Duncan gulped as he realized the terror those surfers must have suffered being in the water with a pack of these ferocious creatures devouring them with such speed.

"The boy's got brains," Lucky replied.

As quickly as the action had started it ended. There was nothing left of the bull but his blood with left streaks in the ocean water. Lucky, Angie and Duncan all sat down in the boat as the water was now still below the boat.

"What's the thing about sharks . . . they always go back there," Lucky said looking down into the deep, unforgiving ocean.

"Yes, but then they always come back looking for their next meal," Duncan replied.

"Yea, they always come back. On that you can depend," Lucky said, as his eyes remained peeled on the ocean's surface. "They will always be hungry again."

CHAPTER 12

11:58 AM:

While the four of them were waiting on the boat to see if there was going to be any more action, the boat was hit hard from below. Stog, who was standing checking his camera, was knocked to the floor by the hit on the boat. Angie fell against Duncan whose hand caught her by her breast and one shoulder.

"Are you okay?" Duncan asked her as his hand held her breast.

"Yes, fine," she said as she pulled her body away from his grip.

"The guys must still be hungry," Lucky said.

"Are you sure about this boat thing?" Duncan again asked Lucky.

"Yea, I'm sure. I've been out here hundreds of times and no shark has ever taken a boat down," Lucky replied sarcastically. "But, I guess we can head back, if you're worried."

"No, I trust . . . your judgment," Duncan felt forced to say.

"So, you're putting your life in my hands?" Lucky asked grinning with his yellow-stained teeth.

Duncan smiled even though he didn't feel like smiling. Again another shark knocked against the bottom of the boat.

"They're really rocking and rolling down there," Lucky said as the four humans sat quietly looking around the boat for any signs of a fin in the water. No one said anything for the next few minutes as a silence sat in the boat waiting to see if there would be any more hits. After five minutes, there was nothing.

Lucky got up and said, "Well, now that's all the fun's over, I guess we can head back."

Lucky tried the engine, but it didn't start. Again he turned the key, but the engine refused to turn over. As Lucky again tried to turn the engine over, the boat was again hit. Both Angie and Stog now looked at Lucky. Their faces betrayed their fear.

"Looks like we got a problem," Lucky reluctantly said.

"I think I'll go below and call the Coast Guard."

"Do you think the engine's dead?" Duncan asked.

"I don't know. Maybe the hits we've been taking has wreaked the blades or disconnected something. I can fix it once we get to the dock, but I'm not too anxious to go in that water right now."

Duncan looked down at the dark water. There was nothing to be seen. No tale tells fin protruding out of the water. No great jaws plunging out from the ocean depths. The sea was even calm as a few waves lapped against the side of the boat. Even the hits had stopped for several minutes leaving a eerie silence.

No, I wouldn't want to be in that water for anything in the world, Duncan thought.

"I think I'll go below and call the Coast Guard. Why don't you come down below with me Duncan," Lucky suggested. "These are your cronies we're calling. Maybe they'll come a little quicker if we tell them you're on board."

Duncan went with Lucky into the tiny chamber below. Once below in the cabin Lucky pulled out a bottle of bourbon. Most of the liquor in the bottle was gone. Lucky took a swig.

"Want some?" Lucky asked holding the bottle out to Duncan.

"No, thanks," Duncan said making an effort to grin.

Lucky then focused his attention on the radio and Duncan sat next to him.

On the deck, Angie sat down across from Stog. He was still looking at his camera for damage from the fall.

"Is it alright?" Angie asked him.

"Yea, I think so. But I've got to be careful with this baby. She cost me plenty. But she's worth it. You can put her in the water and she's still okay," he said as his stumpy fingers caressed the hard steel.

"Well, nobody takes pictures like you," Angie reassured the man sitting across from her.

Stog didn't notice the compliment but stood up with one leg on the side of the boat, he was focusing the camera when the boat was again hit from below. Stog and his camera were plunged into the ocean.

Angie ran to the side to see if Stog was all right. Or if to see if a shark was anywhere in site. She could only see Stog flapping his large arms in the water. But he was not swimming to the boat, but away from it.

"Stog, what are you doing?" Angie cried out to him.

"My camera," he spurted out as the ocean water lapped in his mouth.

A few feet from Stog was his camera floating on the surface of the sea.

"Jesus Christ, Stog. That was a shark that hit us. Get back here. Forget about your camera."

Stog kept swimming toward the camera. Angie's eyes scanned the water for any sign of a shark. She could see nothing but Stog and his camera. Stog had finally reached his camera and with an effort was swimming back toward the boat.

"Hurry up, Stog, hurry up. Oh, please God, make him hurry," Angie prayed as she looked for sharks.

Finally Stog reached the boat. As his one hand held on to the side of the boat, he handed Angie his camera.

"Oh, Stog how stupid can you be," she reprimanded him as she took the camera from him. "You could have gotten eaten out there."

"Naw, I'm not good shark bait. I stink too much," Stog said as Angie bent down to offer her hand to help him lift his body out of the water. Angie was holding on to both of his arms as she tried to lift him out of the water. Stog was heavy and his foot was trying to find the side of the boat. He tried to push against to boat to lift himself up when his foot slipped back into the water. Angie again grabbed his arms and leaned backwards in a effort to pull Stog into the boat. Angie was holding on Stog's arms and was just about to call out to Lucky and Duncan for help when Stog's body was lifted up by a force from the water. A Great White had Stog's body clear up to his waist and had pushed Stog nearly level with the boat. Angie grabbed Stog firmly by the arms as the shark firmly held the man's hips with its teeth. Angie was on one side and the Great White was on the other and they were in a game of tug of war with Stog in the middle. The shark then bit clear though Stog's body taking the lower half of Stog's body with it as it swam below the water's surface. In a moment the shark was gone and Angie pulled what was the rest of Stog's body into the boat. She fell backwards and Stog's body fell on top of her. By some quirk, Stog was still breathing. His breaths were hoarse as blood poured from his mouth as he laid on top of Angie.

Lucky and Duncan had heard the commotion when Angie was fighting with the shark over Stog's body. They ran up the stairs. When Lucky and Duncan emerged from below, they found Angie sprawled on the floor with half of Stog's body on top of her.

"What happened?" Lucky asked startled at the site.

"My God," Duncan said as he viewed Stog's intestines lying on the boat's floor.

Angie was crying. Her body were covered with blood, as Stog's body lay on the floor of the boat with her. Her hair, a few moments before pulled back in a tight ponytail, now hung loosely around her face and was dripping with blood.

Lucky pulled Stog's body, which by now had stopped breathing, off of Angie. Lucky put his face next to Stog's to see if there was any breathing. Angie was crying hysterically her legs pushing Stog's corpse away from her.

"Get her below," Lucky shouted to Duncan.

Duncan stepped over the remains of Stog's body to pick up Angie. She seemed unwilling to leave a first as she pushed both of his hands away as he tried to help her up.

"Come on Angie," Duncan said in a gentle voice as he knelt down next to her to help her up. She allowed herself to be helped.

CHAPTER 13

12:07 PM:

When Duncan took her below to the cabin, Angie exploded.

"That fucking shark. I'm going to kill it," she yelled as she threw her body on the bench.

"Angie, please, calm down," Duncan tried to reason with her.

"No, I'm not going to calm down. I'm never going to calm down again."

"Come on, Angie. This is just business. This is your business. This isn't personal, we're on a job here."

"Oh, no, it's personal. It's very personal now. When that shark ripped Stog from my hands, it personal," she said.

"When I went to the hospital and saw those boys with their legs and arms missing—that was business. But when that shark and I fought over Stog's body—that was personal. It was between me and that shark. And that shark might have won, but I'm going to get him . . . and everyone of his kind."

"Angie, what are you saying? Listen to yourself."

"I know exactly what I'm saying. I saw the enemy today," she said with determination in her eyes. "And he had no pity. He surveyed and he stalked. And then he killed. He killed with intent and maliciousness. And I will do the same."

"Angie, you've been through a lot today . . . to see a man die like that . . . it must have been horrible. You're just in shock, you don't know what you're saying," Duncan tried to reason with her.

"I know exactly what I'm saying. I am an officer in the United States Navy and it's my job . . . it's my job to defend our population from any enemy force. And that is the enemy out there," she said pointing to the side of the boat.

"Angie, they're not our enemy. They're just a bunch of sharks. They've been around for millions of years. Longer than we've been here."

"Yea, that's what I used to think. But they're different now. Now they're capable of more than we ever realized. They're smarted than you think. They know enough to stalk and hunt in packs. I don't think the incident with the surfers will be the last. They found a good feeding ground, and now they're just looking for another. We're just waiting here and there's nothing we can do about it."

"Angie, you're crazy," Duncan said as he was amazed at Angie's anger.

"I'm not crazy, I'm not crazy," Angie said as she rubbed her forehead with both of her hands clenched into fists.

"Listen, we're getting out of here in a moment. We got hold of the Coast Guard and they're on their way. You need to get a hold of yourself before they come. If they see you like this . . ." Duncan said as he sat down next to Angie on the bench.

Angie looked up at him. She knew what he was talking about. That she had to pull herself together before anyone saw her. Duncan was on her side.

"You're right," she said finding some of her composure.

"We'll talk about all this later, when we're alone," he said to her. "But you don't want to talk about the United States Navy fighting a bunch of sharks in front of . . . in front of everyone."

She nodded her comprehension.

"You're gonna be fine," Duncan said as his hand reached up to brush some of Angie's hair from her face. Angie's hand calmly reached up and she held on to Duncan's hand for a moment.

"Are you better now?" he asked her.

"Yea, sure," she replied as Lucky stuck his head down into the cabin.

"The Coast Guard's here," he told them.

"Great, let's go, Angie,' Duncan said as he helped Angie up. "Let me get your hair pulled back," he said as he pulled Angie's blood stained hair back off her face.

CHAPTER 14

12:37 PM:

Back at the dock Angie ran up the hill leaving Lucky to deal with the Coast Guard and the depositing of what was left of Stog's body. Duncan started to follow her, calling after her as she ran up the hill. But Angie was on pure adrenalin now and she seemed to possess super human power that whisked her up the mountain.

"Let her go," Lucky said to him as Duncan started to make his way up the hill. "She's just a woman, after all. Can't handle the emotional stuff."

Duncan gave Lucky a hard look, a look Lucky noticed.

"Don't get stuck on her man. She's nothing but trouble," Lucky said to Duncan. "All women are trouble one way or another."

Duncan ignored the remark and ran up the hill after Angie. He wasn't about to let some old hippie tell him how to run his life.

She was sitting inside the rental car on the passenger side.

As he opened the car door, she said, "Let's go."

"Where?" he asked.

"Anywhere. Just go. Get me away from this place."

Duncan nodded and drove. They crossed the Golden Gate bridge, drove through the streets of San Francisco and headed over the Oakland bridge to the East Bay. Angie said nothing. Neither did Duncan. The dry hills of the lands east of the San Francisco bay formed their bleak passageway. As they headed out the highway toward Yosemite, Duncan finally said, "How far do you think we should go? New York?"

"Very funny," she said sarcastically.

"Seriously, Angie, we can't run away from this. What are we going to do next?" he asked her as the car's wheels sped away from the ocean.

"I don't know. I just needed to get away for a while. I know what I have to do. I have to go back to face . . . all this. That's my job, isn't it? Isn't that what you told me?" she said as look at the asphalt of the road rushing by.

"Yea. It's late. Let's get a hotel and go get drunk," Duncan suggested.

"Yea, whatever," Angie said as she stared at the dry hills of California.

Duncan examined the woman sitting next to him with the blood stained clothes. She was nothing like the Lt. Reynolds who showed up at his office yesterday with her white suit and demanding questions. She was a lost woman dealing with her incapability of having complete control over her world. She wanted control over everything that could effect her life—even sharks that roamed the open ocean.

Angie said nothing, but looked ahead at the barren highway in front of her.

"I think we should stop and get you some new clothes," Duncan suggested. "If you walk into a hotel looking like that, they'll think you're part of a hacked team."

"Yea," Angie replied only half listening to him. Maybe she was part of a hacked team she thought to herself.

At Pleasanton Duncan spotted the big clear sign of a K-Mart.

"Hey, there's a K-Mart. Isn't that where American shops?" he said in a voice that was trying to be light.

Angie said nothing as she looked at the large red letters.

"I know it's not quite the posh style you're probably used to, but . . ."

"It's fine," she said.

Duncan ran into the store, picked up a pair of jeans and a t-shirts, a sweatshirt and some underwear for Angie. He also picked up some clothes for himself as his uniform had smears of blood on it from when he helped Angie on the boat.

When he returned to the car, Angie got into the back seat to change. Duncan had driven around to the back of the store, but he kept his eyes peeled for any onlookers. He couldn't help himself from looking once in the rear view mirror. He could see Angie's torso, from the neck to her breast as she held her arms up to pull on a t-shirt.

"I forgot the bra," he said as she pulled the t-shirt down to cover her loose breasts.

"I'll survive," she said.

When she was dressed Angie stuffed her bloody clothes into the K-Mart bag. Duncan then stood outside as he removed his shirt and his pants and put on the new pair of jeans. Angie looked outside the window at Duncan's torso, his muscular tan body finely lined with muscles. He was a man who took care of his body by running regularly along Palm Park in Santa Barbara.

"Not bad for a Coast Guard," she said to him as he got back into the car.

"Not bad yourself for a naval officer," he replied.

The two drove a little bit farther into the farmland of California's central Valley. Off the 5 they found a little motel. It's long patio housed eight connected units.

"Shall we get one room or two?" he asked her as she got out of the car.

Angie looked at him a long time before answering, "One is okay."

After they checked in, Duncan and Angie walked to the room. Duncan opened it to reveal a small room, clean with one double bed.

Angie looked inside and said, "I've got to take a shower."

She disappeared into the bathroom before Duncan even had time to say anything. Duncan laid down on the bed thinking of Angie. She was there in the bathroom. She was only a few feet away from him, naked. He imagined her naked body being hit by the water of the shower. He imagined her smiling at him as the water fell down her throat to her breasts. He imagined her stomach and the water falling down her legs. When the water turned off, he waited for her to come out. He imagined she would be naked. He wanted her naked. But when Angie did come out of the bathroom, she was dressed and her hair was in a towel.

"I'm hungry," she said not even noticing Duncan was lying on the bed. "Let's go eat."

They found a little Mexican place down the road. They sat down in one of the dark booths where the seats were covered in red nogahide. Duncan ordered Menudo, followed by a beef enchilada. Angie ordered a burrito. Both ordered Margaritas. An hour later, both were smashed with three margaritas each. They hardly talked at all that night. Neither of them could let go of the scene with Stog today and it haunted their meal. They concentrated on drinking their margaritas as though it would relieve them of their thoughts.

With an effort, Duncan drove back to the hotel. When he opened the door, Angie walked straight in and plopped herself face down on the bed. She did not move again for eleven hours.

CHAPTER 15

8:03 AM:

The next morning Duncan woke up to hear Angie talking in a sweet, little girl voice on the phone.

"Hey, it's me . . . No, I'm just fine. I had a bad day yesterday, that's all. I needed to get away from it all . . . I'm fine today, I'm all right, really I am. I just needed a good night's sleep. I'll see you later."

Duncan pretended to be asleep as he listened to Angie's phone call. He imagined she was calling her lover, her boyfriend, her whatever you call it these days . . . her significant other. Wow, just think human beings were being labeled as 'significant others' as if that actually meant something. After Angie hung up the phone, she went into the bathroom. Duncan could hear the shower running. No, not the shower, it was the bath. What a crazy woman that was in the bathroom, he thought. He wondered if she would have slept with him if she hadn't passed out. She certainly gave him every indication that she was willing. She was a flirt. A military official. A manic woman covered with blood. She was a million things, but all those things were not available to him. She had a significant other.

He waited sitting on the bed until she got out of the bathroom.

"Hope you didn't use all the hot water," he said as she came out her hair up in a towel. She had washed her hair again even though she had washed it the night before.

"No, but I used both of the towels. Sorry," she said handing him one of the wet towels. "I didn't know whether you would want to take a shower or not this morning."

"No, I prefer the smell of sweat and blood and a day's drive in the desert on me," he said.

"You don't smell that bad to me," she said. "I kind of like it."

There she goes flirting again, Duncan thought. Women, you can never figure them out.

After Duncan showered and dressed the two headed back to San Francisco. Duncan didn't talk much in the car on the way back. He had some self-respect, after all, and he wasn't about to let Angie think she could use him or have him whenever she wanted.

"Where are we going?" he finally asked her when they reached Pleasanton.

"Back to Lucky's," she said. "I talked with him this morning on the phone."

"You called Lucky this morning? When?" he asked her.

"I called him before you woke up."

"Did you call anyone else?"

"No."

"That was him on the phone?"

"Yea."

"Oh," Duncan replied. Maybe he didn't know Angie as well as he thought. For the rest of the ride Duncan tried to pick up a conversation with Angie, but she was intent on looking out window at the passing cars as though that would solve her problems.

They reached Lucky's house at about eleven o'clock. Lucky was reading the paper with his legs up on his desk as if nothing had happened the day before.

"So any news?" Angie asked as she walked into Lucky's room. "Yea, there's a mention of the attack in the paper. You know they're always going to pick up on the gore and guts."

"Did they make any connection with the surfer attack?" Angie asked him.

"No, not yet. But they will."

"How can they make a connection?" Duncan asked. "They weren't at all connected."

"In the public mind, all shark attacks are related," Lucky replied.

"The national papers will put the incidents together—Killer sharks threatened the California coast or something like that," Angie said.

"But there was only one guy yesterday," Duncan said.

"Yea, there's no relation. We all know that. Yesterday was just a freak accident. But the surfer thing . . ."

Lucky said.

"What do you think we should do?" Angie asked Lucky.

"What do I think WE should do?" Lucky replied. "There's no WE about this. It's your thing."

"I have to report what I think is happening. That's why I was sent out here," Angie said.

"And what do you think the United States government is going to do about this?" Lucky asked.

"Whatever they have to do," Angie replied without missing a beat. She was back in form. The woman who had broken down yesterday with the half-eaten body lying in her arms was gone. As was the drunken woman lying on the bed last night. Lt. Reynolds of the United States Navy was back and in form.

"Whatever?" Lucky said as he threw the paper down on his desk.

"Yes, whatever needs to be done, will be done," she replied in a military manner.

"And what if that includes destroying the entire shark species," Lucky baited her.

"I doubt it will go that far."

"But if it does?" Lucky continued his questioning.

"If it does, it does," Angie said not wanting to admit her feelings or her plans to Lucky.

"Angie, you're headed into dangerous waters here. I know you can recommend anything you want, and they might listen to you."

"Yes, they might," she confirmed.

"You're not going to propose anything too drastic are you?"

"I don't know what I'm going to propose yet. But I've got twenty-two dead people in Santa Barbara."

"You know Stog isn't part of them. He's not part of that problem."

"I know."

"Don't let what happened yesterday to Stog affect what your thinking. The sharks that attacked those boys were something different. Stog was just a freak accident."

"Don't you think I know that? Why do you keep harping on it?"

"Because your decision could affect hundreds of sharks. The species is already endangered. Are you willing to recommend that they are wiped out entirely because of a few dead boys."

"Twenty-two. There were twenty-two dead boys, Lucky," Angie shouted at him. She caught her anger before she said anything else. She said in a softer voice, "If it's a one-time thing, then it's a one-time thing. But if it isn't . . ."

"If it isn't, you're going to recommend their destruction," Lucky said.

"At least the group responsible."

Duncan looked at her with her cold-like manner. She was a professional. She would stop at nothing to get the job done.

"Maybe there's a reason these sharks are attacking now," Duncan interjected into the conversation. He felt he had to come between Lucky and Angie somehow.

"What do you mean?" Lucky asked.

"Well, these sharks off the Santa Barbara coast may be looking for new feeding grounds because two years back the seal population on the Channel Islands was devastated by starvation. Literally thousands of them died," Duncan said.

"I remember that," Lucky replied.

"Yea, it was quite a problem for us. The beaches were literally full of dead pups. We pushed them into the sea."

"Providing a easy feeding ground, which may have allowed the shark population to grow," Lucky theorized.

"And then afterwards with the larger shark population, there was not the regular feeding grounds, which they were used to feeding off of," Duncan pointed out. "Now, there are no adult seals to feed off of."

"So, now the regular feeding grounds of the sharks no longer exist," Angie said, "because of the baby seals that died two years ago don't exist as adults."

"Yes. Now you have a healthy population of Great Whites sharks with nothing to eat. Of course, they're going to look for a new food source," Lucky replied. "These sharks may have evolved into a specialized hunters that hunt like a team for a more efficient kill. It could be a evolutional process."

"And that source of food is now humans," Duncan replied.

"Well as far as a shark is concerned, humans are rather inept in the water. They are easy prey," Lucky noted. "Up to a hundred years ago there were virtually few human beings along the California coast. It wasn't really worth it for them to go after humans because there were so few."

"But today," Angie theorized, "there are millions of humans in California. The ocean is full of them—swimming, surfing, diving. In a way it only makes since for the sharks to now look to human beings as prey."

"But is it ethical for us to interfere with nature?" Duncan questioned the group. "With a basic evolutional process."

"When that process involves the destruction of citizens of the United States government . . . Yes," Angie replied without hesitation.

CHAPTER 16

11:23 AM:

"We got to go," Angie suddenly announced.

Duncan looked at her surprised that they were already leaving Lucky's house so quickly after they arrived. Certainly they hadn't driven three hours just for that little chat.

"Sure," Lucky said as he remained in his chair. He gave Angie a hard look. His eyes showed his frustration, but his body remained relaxed. He tossed his pencil hopelessly down on his desk.

Once in the car, Duncan asked Angie, "What was that about?"

"I just didn't want to stay there and get into it with Lucky. I know his position," she said.

"His position?" Duncan asked.

"Yea. Lucky will do anything to save the Great Whites. He hates all this because he knows the public will go crazy now. They'll be a bunch of cowboys now out in their fishing boats trying to catch the sharks. They might even lift the band of catching Great Whites because of this. And Lucky's right. They are an endangered species."

"But you want to kill them too," Duncan asked as Angie took a curve a little to quickly. She made a good recovery and her driving did not affect for conversation.

"No, I don't. But I don't want another attack like the one in Santa Barbara."

"No," Duncan concurred remembering the bloody coastline after the first attack. "So where were are we going now?"

"I need to contact Washington. And we need to rent of couple of hotel rooms in San Francisco for the night," she said.

Duncan noticed Angie's desire to rent a couple of rooms. Maybe he had missed his chance. Maybe he should have done something last night. On the way to San Francisco, as they drove through the streets to the hotel, Duncan could think of nothing but Angie's naked breasts, which he had seen in the car when she changed her clothes yesterday.

They checked into the Hilton in San Francisco. Angie gave her credit card to pay for both the rooms.

"You don't have to do that," Duncan said as they took the elevator up to their floor.

"It's a business expense. You're part of my business here," she said not looking at him.

They got off the elevator together and walked to their separate rooms down the hall from each other.

"Why don't you rest awhile," Angie instructed Duncan. "I've got a few phone calls to make. I'll call you when I'm through. We'll get something to eat then."

Inside his room, Duncan took off his shirt and laid on the bed. He flipped on the TV with the remote control. There was an old movie on the channel. It was Judy Garland in Meet Me in St. Louis. He watched a few moments of it as Judy was singing 'Have yourself a merry little Christmas' while his mind blanked out from the previous few days. A few minutes later, he turned the channel. There was a news report.

The announcer said, "We have it confirmed of another massive shark attack off the California coast. In Santa Monica, several swimmers were attacked and allegedly eaten by a group of great white sharks . . ."

Duncan's heart beat fast as he pulled himself to the edge of the bed. The camera was focused on a long shot of the beach with a clear view of the Santa Monica pier. There was nothing to see, but Duncan was grateful they could not show the gore he knew was involved in a great white shark attack. Duncan flew out of his room and ran down the hall in his bare feet to Angie's room. He knocked frantically on the door. There was no answer. He pounded the door with his fists.

"Damn, Angie," he said, "don't be taking another shower. I'm the one who should be taking a cold shower."

Angie answered the door with a phone in her hand. Her face showed her irritation at his interruption.

"There's been another attack," he said to explain his being there. Angie ignored him and continued talking on the phone as she waved him away. He ripped the phone from her hand.

"There been another shark attack. In Santa Monica. It's on the TV now," he said pushing pass her to turn on the television. He flipped the channels until he found one with a photograph of a great white shark. Angie kept the phone in her hand, listening to the report.

A man voice said on the television, ". . . It's been confirmed that there are several fatalities. The attack is obviously connected with the Santa Barbara killings just a few days ago as California suffers another attack from sharks . . ."

"Oh, shit," Angie said into the phone. "It's on the television right now. There's been another attack. Have you heard anything about it? Yes, it looks like several victims."

Angie listened to the voice on the other end. Every once in a while Duncan could hear her replies, "Yes, sir." "I understand." "Yes, sir."

She finally hung up the phone.

"What did he say?" Duncan asked her.

"We're going to San Diego," Angie said.

"San Diego?"

"Well, first we're going to Los Angeles to check out this attack. But then we're going to San Diego . . . to the Navy Base there. We're going have debrief these . . ."

"Debrief? What are you planning?" Duncan asked.

"We're committed now. I have my orders," Angie replied. A hard look came over her face.

"Committed? To what?"

"We are going to find these sharks and destroy them," Angie replied.

"What do you mean WE? I'm not part of you . . . of your organization. My jurisdiction ends in Santa Barbara."

"I mean we, Duncan," she said firmly.

"I hardly think you need me. It sounds like you have the entire US Navy helping you."

"But I need you. I can trust you. Yesterday on the boat, when I was going a little crazy, you made me calm down. You knew I couldn't go out there and make a fool of myself in front of everyone."

"I'm sure you would have done the same for me," Duncan replied.

"I don't know if I would have. I don't know if I would have cared enough to try. But yesterday, I knew you were on my side. I knew I could trust you."

Duncan stood there dumb-faced as Angie spoke.

"And then last night, when we were alone in the hotel room and I was drunk," she continued to say, "you could have done anything, and I would have let you . . ."

"Damn," Duncan said in a low voice to himself.

"But you didn't. You treated me all right. I know I can trust you. I know you can help me."

"Angie, I don't understand you at all," Duncan finally said.

"You don't have to understand me. You only need to help me," she replied.

"Help you? Help you what?"

"Find these sharks. Find them and kill them," she said without hesitation.

"Hey, Angie, this is way out of my field. I'm just a guy in the Coast Guard who lives in a little nice town on the coast. I don't know anything about sharks."

"No, but you know how to make the right decision."

Duncan looked up at the ceiling. He did not want to go with Angie. She was a kooky girl and fighting 5,000 pound monsters wasn't in his job description.

"I'm not going," he finally said.

"Oh, yes, you are. I've already cleared it with your commander," she replied without missing a beat.

"When did you do that?" he asked not believing her.

"It was the first call I made when I got to my room. You're mine, now. At least until this is over."

"You mean, I'm actually reporting to you," he asked.

"Something like that."

"Shit," he said not trying to hide his dislike.

"Now, are you sorry you didn't do anything with me last night."

He gave her a long look, but didn't answer.

"Then, let's go to the airport. I'm going to call Lucky to meet us there."

"You're taking Lucky along too?" Duncan asked surprised because just an hour before Angie seemed so anxious to get away from Lucky.

"Of course, he is the world's foremost expert on Great Whites sharks."

CHAPTER 17

2:32 PM:

When Angie and Duncan arrived at San Francisco airport the reports of the shark attack had already swept the news. It was the only thing people were talking about. As they sat in the airport lounge, Duncan could hear a man talking about his encounter with a shark.

"I was surfing in Hawaii. I looked down and there he was. His mouth was wide-open ready to take a bite out of my leg. Thank god, I just stayed on my board . . ." the man told his woman companion.

Angie seemed preoccupied and didn't talk as they waited for the plane. When they boarded the plane, Lucky still had not arrived. The door of the airplane was just being closed and then was reopened. Lucky came strutting back as if he had all the time in the world.

"You didn't think they'd leave without me, did you?" he asked Angie and Duncan as he took a seat across from them in business class.

"This is serious," Angie said as though she had to remind Lucky they were not going on vacation.

"All of life is serious, Angie. Everything is serious to someone. This chair is a serious business to the designer. This magazine is a serious business to the publisher. So what do you know?" Lucky changed from his philosophy of life to the business at hand without a stutter.

"Not now," Angie said in a low voice. "In the car to the site."

Without another word, Lucky picked up the American Airlines magazine and began to read an article that Duncan noticed was on Cajun cooking.

In the car, Duncan drove out to Santa Monica while Angie talked to Lucky who was sitting in the back seat.

"I got my orders. After I make an appraisal of the latest attack, we'll be heading down to San Diego to the Navy base. They have a team of divers."

"Are you going into hand to hand combat with the sharks?" Lucky asked sarcastically.

"Lucky, you're here as an advisor. You know sharks. We need your expertise on this matter. I know your opinion in this matter. I assure you I sympathize with you. But I've got a pack of sharks out there, and they are routinely attacking our beaches and killing people. People are afraid to go into the water. What are we going to do? Close down all the beaches. And then what? What if they start attacking boaters, divers, surfers, swimmers, kyackers . . . I've got a whole bunch of people to protect."

"At what cost? Are you going to annihilate every life form that threatens the human race? They've been around a lot longer than we have," Lucky said in defense of his beloved sharks.

Angie let out a sigh of tiredness. "I know, I know, Lucky. But we cannot control them. We cannot predict when they will attack next. We could boycott every beach in the world, but we have no way to trace them. They can attack anywhere, anytime. We need to take control of the situation."

"And control for you is death," Lucky said.

Angie said nothing else but looked out of the car to the lanes of Santa Monica Freeway in L.A.

When they arrived at the beach in Santa Monica, it was already a media frenzy.

"Those poor guys haven't got a chance," Lucky said as they made their way through the crowd. Angie was leading the group as Lucky and Duncan followed her.

"What poor guys do you mean?" Duncan took a chance and asked Lucky.

"The sharks. It's all over for them now. Who Angie doesn't kill, these guys will."

The three of them crossed over the police line to view the beach. Other than the fact there was no one on the beach but a few Coast Guards and police, it didn't look any different. The blood in the ocean was already swept away.

Near the car of the police, Angie and the others were briefed on the incident.

"Thirty-seven people are believed to be dead. We can't confirm this because . . . well, we don't have the bodies," the police officer told them. "Another four were seriously maimed. One woman lost her leg. A kid lost this arm. Two teenagers were attacked but not killed. The part of the beach between the south side of the pier toward Muscle Beach was packed with maybe a hundred or two hundred people. It's the Santa Ana winds and this blasted hot summer were having. Even with the threat of sharks, they still come here in droves from the valleys to go in the ocean. There were lots of witnesses. We took them all down to the armory for questioning."

"And what are they saying happened? Did anyone see them coming," Angie questioned the man.

"No, no one noticed a thing. Some people say a queer silent preceded the attack. But it was definitely a pack of them."

"Any guess on how many?" Angie asked.

"Generally we're hearing reports of around twenty-five, maybe thirty sharks," the officer reported.

"And how long did the attack last?" Angie asked.

"I would guess not more than five minutes. Most of the people did not even have a chance to get out of the water before the sharks were gone as quickly as they came."

A fleet of Navy and Coast Guard ships from San Diego could now be seen as they approached from the south. They made their way toward the few Coast Guard boats already stationed off the coast that came up from San Pedro.

"Looks like the United States Navy is here to save the day," Lucky smirked as he watched the flotilla of boats making their way north.

"But too late to do any good," Duncan said as he looked at his comrades arriving in full force. "I wonder if that's what it was like with the Indians. If the cavalry just came too late to do any good."

Lucky laughed at what Duncan had said and replied, "They could always count the dead."

"We can hardly even do that," Duncan said.

The three made their way to the armory to interview the witnesses. But there was not much to decipher. Angie, Duncan and Lucky each took a group of about twenty-five people and listened again and again to the reports of the carnage that had occurred a few hours before. The pattern of the attack was similar in many ways to the attack in Santa Barbara. This attack occurred later in the morning at 10:34. But the beach was already full as a Santa Ana was blowing in from the desert for the past couple of days and the temperature in L.A. had surged to 110 degrees in the valley and even to the 90's near the beaches. The sharks came in, attacked the victims and quickly left. It was 6:00 by the time the three had finished with the interviews. They got in the car for the three-hour drive to San Diego.

CHAPTER 18

6:03 PM:

On their drive down to San Diego that evening, they stopped at Seal Beach for a bite to eat. The beaches were deserted despite the fact it was over 100 degrees in the valleys that day and the sun had still not set in the west. No one was going in the water now.

"How fast can a shark swim?" Duncan asked as they sat in a booth overlooking the ocean.

"About fifty miles a day," Lucky replied without hesitation, before he bit into his tuna sandwich.

"Fifty miles," Duncan repeated calculating in this mind a diagram of the area that the sharks could be in. "That makes them somewhere between here to the south and Ventura to the north, right now."

"That's why we have to act quickly," Angie said. "We've got to track them now, while we know approximately where they are. Let's go. We got work to do."

As Angie marched to the cashier to pay the bill, Lucky gathered a few of the cracker packages and stuffed them into his pockets. As Duncan was looking at him, Lucky said, "I sometimes I get hungry at night and where we're going . . . well you can't go to the refrig for a midnight meal."

When they arrived at the Navy base in San Diego, they were lead into a meeting already in progress. A colonel was addressing the group. There was a large diagram on the screen outlining the California coast with an area marked off in red approximately the same area that Duncan described at dinner as the area the sharks should still be in.

". . . tomorrow at five hundred hours, we leave here to travel north to this area," the colonel said as the three took their seats in the rear of the room. "It has been determined that the enemy is in this area."

Duncan frowned that the sharks were now being termed as the enemy.

"Our divers will position themselves approximately every mile along this front. We will cut off their escape from the north, south and west. And unless the guys can now walk on land, we've got them. Lt. Reynolds, one of our shark specialists, has just joined us. She will brief you on shark behavior."

Angie walked up to the podium and began her stories of the sharks, starting with the assault on the USS Indiana. Lucky followed her talk with one of his own on the behavior patterns of Great White sharks. His Hawaiian shirt stuck out in the room of white.

By 11:00 that night, everyone was in their quarters for the night. They tried to sleep as they waited for the 4:30 call in the morning when they would go out into the ocean to face the sharks.

CHAPTER 19

4:34 AM:

The next morning, Duncan, Angie and Lucky went out on one of the Navy's boats. About fifty boats had been sent out with about 500 divers. The larger ships that were sent up yesterday where used as posts between the smaller boats. The divers were sent down in shark cages, while the boat crew looked for signs of any sharks on the surface. Each boat was within one mile of the next, until a line was formed along the California coast and the open sea.

Duncan was sure the sharks would be caught. They had to be in this area. But as the day wore on, there were no sightings. Not of the great whites. A few sharks, tigers and sands were caught, loners in the large nets that the Navy had set up. But there was no pack. There were no great whites.

"What do you think," Angie asked Lucky in the late afternoon.

"I don't know. Despite all this," Lucky said flinging his arms around, "it's still like looking for a needle in a haystack. And who's to say that they travel in a pack. Maybe they only meet for the kills."

"Could they be that intelligent?" Duncan questioned him.

"I don't know how fucking intelligent they are?" Lucky said exasperated at the whole event. "But at this point I'd be willing to believe anything."

CHAPTER 20

7:59 **PM**:

At nineteen hundred hours, the boat Angie, Lucky and Duncan were on began to return to shore. They had spent the day on a small Navy boat watching for signs of the sharks. After the divers came up in the shark cage, their boat made its way back to San Diego. Angie, Lucky and Duncan along with the rest of the crew, except for the driver of the boat, went below. The guys were hungry. As everyone sat down to eat the meal laid out on the table, Angie remembered she left her hat in one of the storage compartments on the deck.

"I'll be back in a minute," she said as she got up from the table. "I forgot my hat upstairs in one of the storage compartments."

"Get in later," Lucky said before he bit into his sandwich.

"No, I think I'll get it now," she said, "while there's still a little light outside. I'm not quite sure which one I put it in and I don't want to be looking for it in the dark."

She went back up the stairs to get it.

After she got her hat, she noticed something in the ocean. The light was already dim as the sun started to set so she couldn't be sure of what she saw or if she saw anything at all. She went toward the back of the boat to look out at the black sea. Her eyes scanned the surface for any sighting of a fin or a movement of water. But she didn't see anything.

"My God, with all this shark stuff I'm starting to see things," she said to herself as she turned around to go back below. At that moment, she glimpse something in the water, close to the boat. Angie was sure she saw something. She turned around and bent over looking into the water. A hit came quick and hard against the boat. Angie fell into the water. The driver of the boat had not even noticed Angie was on deck as he was wearing headphones listening to the Grateful Dead. The boat moved on leaving Angie behind in the black water.

When Angie fell into the ocean she flipped over. Her mouth was full of water and she was disoriented as to where she was. She strove to the surface to find the air. When she surfaced, she was coughing. And then it hit her. Where she was. She looked up to see the boat quickly leaving her behind. And then she remember what caused her to fall into the water. The hit. The hit the boat took that made her fall in could only be caused by one thing. And now she was in the water with it.

She looked up to the sky and started swimming toward the boat. The western sky was now a maze of colors as the sun was setting. She was nowhere near land. Even if there were no shark near her, she would never make it. She knew the boat was maybe ten miles offshore when she fell into the ocean. And night was coming. And she didn't have a life jacket. And she knew a shark was here, near her. At any moment she expected to be devoured. To be eaten. Her eyes tried to scan the water for the telltale fin. But Angie knew, it was the great white's pattern to attack from below. To plunge up from the depths of the ocean and seize it's prey from beneath the water. She didn't have a chance even to know when she would be attacked. And nighttime was the traditional feeding time for sharks. If there's any place you don't want to be, it's in the middle of the ocean, at night, with a great white shark in the area.

Duncan had noticed the hit on the boat, along with Lucky who looked up as the boat rocked back and forth.

"Looks like they want to play again," Lucky said.

"I don't think I like playing with these guys," Duncan replied. "I wonder if Angie's all right."

"Yea, sure," Lucky said taking another bite from his submarine sandwich. A few minutes passed, before Duncan said, "She sure is taking a long time. I think I'll go up and see if she's okay."

"Angie a big girl, she doesn't need you looking after her," Lucky said.

"Still, I think I'll go," Duncan said. On the way up Duncan said to Lucky who couldn't hear him, "She needs me more than you think."

When Duncan arrived on the deck, he could only see the driver with his headphones on.

"Angie, you up here?" he called out.

There was no answer.

"Angie, Angie, where are you?" he called out as he started frantically looking around the boat. The boat wasn't that big. Duncan ran to the driver and ripped the headphones off his head.

"Did you see Angie up here?"

"Who?" the man replied.

"Lt. Reynolds, did you see Lt. Reynolds up here."

"No, nobody has been up here since we started back."

"Stop the boat," Duncan demanded.

"What?"

"Stop the boat, turn the boat around," Duncan agained insisted.

The man looked at him not comprehending his words.

"I think Angie fell overboard."

"What?" replied the man as his small brain could not comprehend that Angie was out there in the ocean and that there was a . . .

At that moment, a faint cry could be heard.

It wasn't an actual word that drifted over the waves to reach their ears, but both men acknowledged the sound of a human voice.

The driver turned the boat back toward the open ocean.

Duncan could make out the form of Angie's head in the dimness of the day.

"Quicker, quicker," he said as his heart beat for Angie. "Every second counts. There's a shark out there with her," he said. At that moment as he saw the black fin scanning the water. It was a race. The fin some fifty feet to the right was heading in the same direction as the boat—toward Angie. The fin disappeared under the surface of the water.

"We're coming Angie, we're coming," Duncan shouted out to her. His eyes diverted toward the spot where the shark had been. "We're almost there. Hold on. You're going to be fine. Really," he said not believing his own words.

The boat pulled along Angie as she started swimming toward the boat. Lucky had run up after hearing the boat turn around and he quickly comprehended the situation.

"Come on Angie, swim," Lucky encouraged her.

A wave pushed into Angie's face as she swallowed the salt water. Her coughing made her stop swimming and tread the water for a moment. Duncan moved toward the boat's brim as if he meant to jump in. Lucky caught him by the arm. "Don't do it, man. We'll have the two of you gone."

Lucky's eyes lead Duncan to the fin about ten feet off the boat. The fin again disappeared below the water's surface. Angie swam until her hand caught Duncan's that was down near the water line. With a single burst of energy Duncan pulled Angie out of the water and into the boat. They both fell on the floor of the boat as Lucky stood looking at the empty jaws of the Great White shark as he jumped out of the water.

CHAPTER 21

8:24 PM:

Duncan quickly took Angie downstairs to one of the small sleeping compartments on the boat. She was shivering from the cold Pacific Ocean water. Angie had not been in the water for more than ten minutes. She was not even close to having hypothermia, but Duncan immediately starting stripping her clothes off of her. Lucky came down as Duncan was removing her blouse, tearing the buttons as he worked to release her from her wet terror.

"Get out of here," Duncan shouted at Lucky. "Keep everyone out of here."

Duncan was afraid Angie might lose it again like she lost it when Stog was killed.

"Cool your pants, Navy boy," Lucky shot back at him, "she'll need some other clothes unless you plan on letting her arrive at the Navy Base stark naked. Of course, that would make a couple of sailor's days. Especially the ones out at sea for six months."

Duncan shot up at Lucky pushing him back with both his hands. "I'm not a Navy boy, you ass-hole. Find something for her to wear and get out of here."

Lucky went to the lockers and found a sailor's uniform. He pulled it out and threw them on the bed ignoring Duncan's anger.

"Here you go. She's gonna be fine. I mean she made it this far. Not too many people can say they were literally rescued from the jaws of death. And it looks like you're the hero. She should be very grateful for that. I imagine she'll show you her appreciation in some way," Lucky said as he smiled at Duncan and left the room.

Duncan pulled off the remaining wet clothes as Angie sat on the bed motionless. He dressed her in the oversized Navy pants and shirt. He found a blanket in one of the cupboards and put it around Angie. Afterwards, Duncan held her in his arms until they pulled into port.

"Don't tell anyone about this," Duncan said to Lucky when Lucky came down to tell him the boat was almost in port.

"What?" Lucky played dumb.

"About Angie. About how close she came to . . ." Duncan whispered to Lucky.

"My friend, there's no way to stop that kind of news. Within a half an hour everyone in port will know."

"They don't have to know how close it was," Duncan said.

"Anytime you're in the water with a shark, it's close. Way too close for most people. Especially if that shark is a Great White."

"She doesn't need the exposure. The questions," Duncan persisted in his protecting Angie.

Lucky looked at Angie. He had known her for about two years. She was a funny woman. Very business like, smart in her own way, and yes, a looker. Lucky wouldn't have minded a roll in the hay with her at that. But she would never do anything with him. But Duncan. He could see them together. Duncan was only a few years older than Angie. And they both worked for the government. It takes a certain type of personality to work for the government. As Lucky scanned Angie's face, she still seemed out of it as if she could not comprehend the language they spoke.

"Hey, Angie, how ya doing?" Lucky said kneeling down to look into her eyes. She didn't even look back, but only stared straight ahead seeing nothing but her own terror. Lucky stood up and said to Duncan, "You know I would never say anything to hurt her. She's a good kid. I hope she's going to be okay."

"Yea," Duncan replied not knowing if she would be okay or not.

As Lucky was walking out the door, he heard Angie say, "I'll be alright, Lucky."

He turned around and found her face, looking at him. Her eyes still had the look of terror in them.

"I know you will, kid. I know you will."

CHAPTER 22

10:09 PM:

Once they were back at the Naval Base Duncan took Angie to her room. He took her clothes off, standard sailor stuff he had put on her after he stripped her of her wet clothes on the boat. He ran her hot water for a bath. He found a small packet of shampoo and poured it into the water so that it made bubbles.

Angie looked at the water. The terror on her face had not left.

"I don't ever want to be in water again," she said as she stood with a towel around her body.

"This is good water. It's hot," Duncan said putting his hand in the water to test its temperature. "And you're still freezing. We need to get your body temperature up. We're inside now. It's only a bathtub. And I'm here."

Angie let him moved her toward the tub as he pulled the towel from around her. As she stood in the tub, he said, "Now, sit down."

Slowly she immersed herself in the hot water. After a while her tense muscles relaxed as the steam from the water fogged up the mirror in the room. Angie began to cry. Duncan knelt next to the tub. With his hand rubbing her back he tried to comfort her.

"You're alright, now, Angie . . . everything's okay. You don't have to go into the water again. It's all over. They aren't going to make you go in the ocean ever again."

After a moment of silence, Angie said weakly, "I have to. It's my job."

Duncan shook his head as he didn't know what to say and he didn't want to debate with Angie after her ordeal today.

That night Duncan again slept in Angie's bed. But she was not drunk like she was the first night sprawled out on the bed. This night she crawled near Duncan, placing her body next to his. On reflex, he put his arm around Angie's shoulder and held her close to his body. Angie placed her head on his shoulder as she sought his protection.

"Try to sleep," he said to her. Angie fell into a restless sleep. Her body flipped about on the bed all night. She cried a little, and mumbled words that Duncan couldn't understand. Duncan did not sleep that night as he watched Angie get through her night of dreaming of sharks and water and helplessness.

CHAPTER 23

8:12 AM:

The next day, the flotilla of Navy boats again headed out to sea as it had done the day before. Angie stayed behind. After breakfast, she took the plane, alone, back to Washington.

"What's going to happen back there?" Duncan asked her as he drove her to the airport.

"There's a meeting with the President," Angie said matter-of-factly.

"The President? Of the United States?" Duncan asked surprised that Angie would be involved in such a high level meeting.

"Yes, the media's been covering this story like crazy. They've turned it into a national threat. The President wants action. Some resolution."

"The President?" Duncan again questioned her.

"Yes, it's not only pressure from the media. The whole world has gone shark crazy. Something's got to be done."

"And you're going to do it?"

Angie looked at him. Her face was blank from any feeling. She was working on batteries. On automatic. The real Angie was left behind in the ocean with the shark.

"Angie, you're not capable of anything . . . not after yesterday. You don't know how close you came to being . . . to not being here today."

"I know how close I was," she said in a steady voice. "I could feel him in the water. He was stalking me. I know I felt his skin against my foot. He was playing with me. That's why I have to do this now."

"Do what? Angie you're crazy. I mean it's normal. You've been under a lot of stress lately. First, Stog and then what happened yesterday."

Angie turned toward him again. Her eyes were dark pools of revenge.

"I have to do what I have to do. I'm the expert. They need a recommendation."

"Angie," Duncan said grabbing her shoulders, "that shark was only doing what it has been doing for thousands of years."

"No," she said shaking her head slowly. "They've changed. They're different now. I don't know if they have always been this smart and they just weren't interested in us as food, or if some evolutional change has occurred. But it's not the same playing field as it has been for millions of years. Things have changed. I don't know if it's us, or them or like you said some freak accident where their food source died, but I do know one thing."

"What's that?" he asked her.

"It's war."

"Is that what you're going to recommend?"

"It's the only thing I can recommend. If we do nothing, they'll be more and more attacks. No one will be able to go into the water. It will be their domain. Can we, as human beings, let that happen?"

"Well, couldn't we just have an agreement that we stay on land and they stay in the water," Duncan said trying to make light of the seriousness of the situation.

"No, not acceptable terms."

"Angie . . ."

"I've got to go Duncan. The plane is waiting."

"The super three-hour coast to coast one?" Duncan asked.

"Yes, something like that. I'll see you when I get back," she said to him.

"I don't know if I'm going to be here," Duncan put out to see what Angie's response would be.

Angie smiled.

"Then I'll find you," she said before she turned and got off of the car.

He watched her as she walked toward the plane the military plane.

After Duncan dropped Angie off at the airport, he was going to drive home to Santa Barbara. It would be a four or five hour trip if there wasn't much traffic. But he would have to travel through Los Angeles and there was always traffic in L.A. Even at two o'clock in the morning the freeways are full of cars in L.A. At the intersection of the 5 for Los Angeles to the north and San Diego to the south, Duncan had to make a split minute decision on which way he would go. At the last moment, Duncan turned south back to the Navy Base.

When he arrived back at the base he went down to the docks and found Lucky who was getting ready to go out again on one of the boats.

"She's gone?" Lucky asked without looking up at Duncan as he walked toward him.

"Yea, she's gone," Duncan said looking out at the sea since he didn't want to look at Lucky.

Lucky looked up from his diving equipment to scan Duncan's face.

"Hey, what's got you, man? Being a Coast Guard in Santa Barbara where one day a bunch of sharks got hungry?"

"Well, that too," Duncan replied.

"But then you fell in love," Lucky said not taking his eyes off of Duncan.

Duncan shook his head negatively.

"I don't think so," Duncan replied.

"Oh, you don't? You got all the symptoms of it, my friend," Lucky persisted in his observations.

"Why do you keep calling me your friend? I'm not your friend. I don't even know you," Duncan retorted angry at Lucky for all the pot shots he had been taking at him during the past few days.

"I may be much more of a friend than you realize," Lucky replied not at all offended by Duncan's attitude.

"I think I'll go back to Santa Barbara," Duncan said as he watched Lucky check his equipment.

"So, you know how to dive," Lucky asked him.

"Sure, of course," Duncan said still angry at Lucky, at Angie and at all of this cramp.

"Want to come down with me today?" Lucky asked.

"Down? You're going diving? Where?" Duncan asked in disbelief that Lucky would want to go diving after what happened to Angie yesterday.

"Down with the big boys?" Lucky replied smiling.

"What are you talking about?" Duncan asked.

"We're going shark hunting today?"

"You're crazy. Now, I know you're crazy. A few days ago, you saw a guy you worked with for years get eaten. And yesterday, Angie almost got it. And now you're going down there . . . with them. What? Do you want to die?" Duncan said.

"We all got to go sometime, my friend," Lucky said simply.

"I'd rather not go in the jaws of some fucking prehistoric shark," Duncan said as he looked out at the ocean.

"I doubt you would be so lucky. You have a better chance on being killed in an auto accident on the way back to Santa Barbara."

"Why would you want to go down there anyway?" Duncan asked.

"Research, my friend, research. And . . . well . . . I guess I just like to scare the shit out of myself once in awhile. There's nothing like meeting a Great White to get your blood flowing," Lucky said.

Duncan said nothing. He didn't want to go. It wasn't that he was afraid, but . . .

"Afraid of the big bad shark?" Lucky asked.

"No, I'm not afraid," Duncan said without missing a beat.

"You just have to do what I do," Lucky said.

"What's that?"

"When you're scared you just start singing . . . It's Seymour," Lucky started singing dramatically, "the friendly white shark. It's Seymour, the friendly white shark. It's Seymour, the friendly white shark. He'll either smile at you or eat you up. Eat you up. Eat you up."

Duncan laughed even though he didn't want to.

"The more scared you are, the louder you sing it," Lucky added before he started singing it at the top of his lungs. When he finished his performance, which was not ignored by the rest of the sailor's on the boat, Lucky said to Duncan, "So are you going to take your chances and go out there with me or are you going to drive back to Santa Barbara? But for my money, it's safer out there."

"Then how come it doesn't look safer?" Duncan asked.

CHAPTER 24

10:44 AM:

Duncan went with Lucky. On the way out, Duncan was fitted with a wet suit and was given some diving equipment. It was state-of-the-art stuff and a lot lighter than Duncan's old equipment which he hadn't even used in three years.

When they reached the site the large shark cage was bought next to the boat. Lucky and Duncan got into the cage as bits of horse meat, tuna and other cut up fish was thrown into the water. For about five miles a mix of blood and guts was trailed behind the boat so every shark within miles would know it was dinnertime. As the cage was lowered into the water, Duncan adjusted his mask so he could see clearly. He looked around both sides half expecting a troop of sharks to be waiting for them in the water with their mouths wide open.

As the cage descended into the cold water, the images of the past week swam before Duncan's eyes. Tales of 5,000 pound sharks, Stog's half-eaten body, Angie in the water with the shark's fin ten feet away. It took everything in him to keep it together. He started to panic. His eyes found Lucky's slightly distorted face behind the mask. Lucky gave him thumbs up. Maybe Lucky was all right after all.

For ten, maybe fifteen minutes, nothing happened. They were lowered twenty feet into the water. Then a single shark appeared. He was big, but not as big as Duncan feared. Maybe thirteen or fourteen footer. Duncan concentrated on his breathing as the giant shark swan toward the cage. His agility in the water was amazing to Duncan.

He had never seen a shark in the water before. As the shark swan by, Duncan looked into the black eye. It was an eye empty of emotion. This creature survived for millions of years on its physical strength and capabilities. Duncan automatically pulled back to the other side of the cage in natural fear of the monster. When Lucky put his hand out to touch Duncan's arm, Duncan jumped up. Lucky pointed behind him. As Duncan turned around, he saw an enormous shark, nearly twice as big as the first one. Its white teeth were showing and it swam toward the cage with its open mouth. Duncan fell back along with Lucky as the gigantic shark hit the cage. Duncan looked up at the small cable that was his lifeline to the boat. That small thin band of steel was the only thing between life and falling into the depths of the Pacific Ocean off the continental divide.

Duncan quickly looked over at Lucky. His face was making strange contortions underneath his mask. Did Lucky go crazy? Was Lucky already crazy? A thrill-seeker who wanted death? And Duncan was with him.

Then Duncan could faintly hear Lucky humming that stupid tune, "It's Seymour, the friendly white shark . . ."

Duncan stared at the crazy man next to him. Then Duncan started humming the tune. He was surprised when it did make him feel better. He felt like he was humming the tune at the top of his lungs as two of the large monsters swam around the cage. Again and again they'd ram the cage, or took swift swims near the two men who were behind the steel bars. Duncan motioned to Lucky to go up. But Lucky shook his head. After another ten or so minutes the sharks left, the horsemeat and tuna eaten, they had other feeding grounds to go to. Lucky signaled the boat to be pulled up.

Duncan wanted to fucking beat shit out of Lucky when they got to the boat. But Lucky said as soon as he pulled off his mask, "Wasn't that cool, man? We could have had them feeding out of our hands."

Duncan didn't say anything he was so angry. He didn't want to lose it in front of the other guys.

When they went down below, Lucky said, "It's always rough the first time. But it gets easier."

"If it's so easy, why were you singing that stupid song," Duncan asked as he pulled the wet suit off.

"Hey man, I'm not saying it's easy. It's just easier. You got to be a real man to go down there and face them."

CHAPTER 25

1:45 PM:

Angie returned to San Diego the next day. Duncan was definitely planning on returning to Santa Barbara when he heard that Angie was already on her way back. He and Lucky waited in one of the bars on the base. It was a functional bar for the sailors and lacked any décor. It had chairs, tables and liquor—that was it. Out of the blue, Lucky said to Duncan, "You did good yesterday."

"What do you mean?" Duncan asked not knowing what Lucky was talking about.

"I mean a lot of guys let the fear get to them. I was down diving with two guys once. This was years ago before we knew much and before we had the shark cages. We three were down near the bottom just scuba diving. It was off the great barrier reef in Australia. I had already made my ascent and was in the boat when one of the guys with me came zooming up out of the water. He was scared shitless. He was also in shock from making his ascent too fast. We were in fifty of so feet of water and he made the trip in about a minute. Of course I was pissed at him. I mean he killed himself. He knew better than to come up so fast. But something down there frightened him. Something that made him so scared he preferred dying to being down there. He died quick like. He wasn't able to say anything before he died so we didn't know what really happened to the other guy. We waited for the other diver for an hour or so. The air in his tank would have been long gone by then. But he never came up. I wanted to go down again, but then

81

we saw the biggest mother-fucking shark we ever saw. I imagine he ate the one guy and that's what sent the other one to his death."

"Shit," was the only thing Duncan could say before taking another slug of this beer.

After drinking their lunch, Duncan and Lucky went back to the office at the base. There was to be another meeting about the shark situation. The two men walked into the large conference room and sat in the back. Angie came in about ten minutes later and walked directly to the podium. As Lucky and Duncan sat in the back of the conference room, they listened to Angie addressed the sea of white suits.

". . . As all of you are already aware, the crisis over the shark attacks in both Santa Barbara and Santa Monica has reached the point of worldwide interest . . . and fear," she began her address to the room of Naval Officers. "It has been recommended by the joint-chiefs-of-staff and the President of the United States that the matter be handled as quickly and efficiently as possible. We are to take all measures to ensure the safety of the people of the United States and in fact, the whole world . . ."

Angie went on but Duncan didn't hear anymore. After a half an hour everyone left the room.

Duncan caught Angie by her arm in the hall, "Can I talk with you?" he asked her in a low voice.

"In a minute," she said rushed. She was not the Angie he knew then. She was Lt. Reynolds looking for a promotion. Duncan waited next to Lucky as Angie made the rounds, talking to the other officers at the meeting.

"I think I'm going to blow," Duncan finally said to Lucky as he was tired of waiting for Angie.

"And miss all this fun. It's wartime baby. The fucking US Navy against the killer whites."

"That's what I mean," Duncan replied. "I don't want to be part of this."

"I don't either. But if we don't stay, who know what they'll do. At least, stick around and sees what happens," Lucky told him.

"I don't know. This is all beyond me now. I'm just some Coast Guard flunky . . ."

"You're alright, Duncan Burton," Lucky said for the first time calling Duncan something other than boy or kid.

Duncan looked at him. He appreciated Lucky late respect for him. Then Duncan looked at Angie as she was talking with animated gestures to a Colonel. Her face was serious. Duncan decided he would wait for her only to tell her goodbye.

After another half an hour, Angie walked over to the two of them sitting outside the conference room.

"Ready to go?" she asked them.

"Where?" Duncan asked. He had somehow forgotten to tell her goodbye.

"I don't know. Somewhere where they aren't talking about sharks," she said.

"Well that precludes anywhere in this world," Lucky said smartly. "Everyone's got the shark fever."

"Well, at least let's get off the base," Angie said as the three walked out of the building toward the car.

"Angie, you can't do this," Lucky said.

Angie didn't respond but walked ahead of the two men with her.

"This is going to be a holocaust and you know it," Lucky challenged her as he walked behind her.

"I don't have a choice here, Lucky," she screamed at him as she turned around to face Lucky. Duncan was surprised by her furious attack. "The President wants the matter contained. It makes us look bad. What are the other countries going to think when we let a pack of sharks attack our coasts and kill our people?"

"You can't just go around killing a bunch of sharks because . . ." Lucky persisted.

"We're not killing all the sharks, just the Great Whites off the California coast. It has been determined that these sharks have developed evolutional advancing practices . . ."

"Angie, you're full of shit. Every time the United States government sees a threat, its answer is elimination. You're no better than Hitler's camps."

"That going a little too far . . ."

"It's how far you are prepared to go that I'm worried about," Lucky said.

"I'll go as far as I need to go," she answered before she again began to walk ahead of two men.

CHAPTER 26

11:22 AM:

During the next week, the three of them waited along with an entire unit of Navy divers and a fleet of ships for the next hit. Angie, after talking with Lucky persuaded her superiors to wait until they could determine the presence of the particular group of great sharks. She convinced her superiors that the sharks responsible for the attacks were a rogue pack and that the majority of Great Whites do not hunt in packs and offers no unusual threat to humans.

There were also the immediate protests of the Animal protection groups and the media, which also called for restraint and not to overreact to the crisis. When the nets were set up after the Santa Monica attack, over 150 dolphins and other animals were killed in the nets. The Animal rights groups went nuts with their campaign against the destruction of sea life along the California coast. Nature and man were pitted against each other. To protect one, the other one had to be destroyed along with innocent victims.

As they waited, Angie, along with Duncan and Lucky went out during the next days to try to spot and tag the great whites along the California coast. It seemed like the only thing they could do at the moment.

On a hot summer's day, Angie, Lucky and Duncan remained below the deck while the boat made its way out to the open ocean. They talked about anything but what was on their minds. When they reached the site, Lucky went up to change into his wet suit. Angie stayed below. She was working on some charts outlining the sites of the attacks. Duncan stayed with her.

"Aren't you going in today?" he finally asked her.

"In?" she asked as if she didn't know what he was talking about.

"Yea, in the water. Aren't you going down with Lucky today."

"No, not today," she answered absentmindedly.

Duncan was relieved that Angie was not going down there. It gave him a reason not to go back down too. He did not relish the idea of returning to the deep cold water of the Pacific with Great Whites ramming his cage. Duncan sat in the corner. He didn't know what to do. Or what to say to the woman who sat across from him.

"Aren't you even going up there to see how things are going?" Duncan finally asked her.

Angie did not seem too interested in what Duncan was talking about. She didn't answer him as her focused remained on the charts.

"What is it with you?" he asked the woman whose eyes were studying maps of the Pacific Ocean near the California coastline.

"What do you mean?" she asked hardly listening to him.

"Yea, you seem to have a love and hate relationship with these sharks. One moment you can't wait to get in the water. And the next, you act like you couldn't care less."

Angie looked straight into his eyes.

"I'm scared to death of them. I always have been. Well, not always. When I grew up in Florida, I was always going to the beach. I used to take my raft out past the breakers and just float for hours. I never even thought about sharks then. Then when I was around twelve years old I went to Sea World with my family. They had on exhibit a Great White. It was a real one caught off of the Bahamas . . ."

"Was it alive?" Duncan asked in disbelief because he had heard that no Great White had ever been kept in captivity.

"No, it was dead. It was kept in a large, refrigerated glass display. But it struck me with fear that something like this was actually swimming around in the ocean. I mean I had seen other shark exhibits, the ones with little eight-footers swimming around in tanks. But this one was different. It was a monster. I never went in the ocean after that. I was so terrified, I would not even go swimming in a pool. I was obsessed with these sharks."

"But how did you get involved in shark research then?" Duncan asked.

"All I could do was think about sharks. I dreamt about sharks. Every night I dreamed of sharks. When I went by the ocean I was always looking for sharks. Then when I was eighteen I decided to go into the Navy. My dad was in the Navy. He was stationed in Orlando at the Training Naval Center before he retired. I grew up on that base. Anyway, I went on an ROTC scholarship. I wasn't planning on doing shark research. But I did know a lot about sharks. My obsessions with them lead me to read about them. One thing led to another. I became a specialist with the Navy. And then I was able to overcome my fear, until . . ."

"Until?" Duncan asked knowing when Angie had lost her nerve.

"Until I saw Stog . . . eaten. Until I started my battle with them. It's like all the fear I had of sharks all my life was coming to a head."

"And then when you were in the water with one of them?" Duncan asked.

"It was like all those dreams I had . . . for years I have been having dreams of sharks. I was always in the water looking at those Great White jaws . . . ready to be devoured."

"But you survived, Angie," Duncan said.

"This time, yes, but what about the next time?" she asked herself. "I don't think I can ever face them again. I don't think I can ever go down there again," she admitted to him.

"Does Lucky know this? Did you tell him?" Duncan asked.

"No. He didn't even ask me if I was going today. He sort of just knew I wasn't. I think he understands. He's faced that fear before."

"And you? When are you going to face that fear?" he asked her.

"Why don't you ask yourself the same question?" she shot back at him.

CHAPTER 27

2:22 PM:

Lucky came up after an hour in the Pacific Ocean. He didn't see any sharks during his descent. They moved the boat three times in an attempt to pick up some scent for the sharks. But they didn't see any that day. When the three of them returned to base in that afternoon the first reports of another attack came in over the radio.

"It's been reported—an attack is currently taking place in the Delta region off the San Francisco Bay," one of the officers on the boat told Angie. Angie ran with the man back to the radio.

"Repeat," Angie said taking the microphone from the operator. The voice on the line repeated the information.

"Send out a helicopter to pick us up right now, we're going to San Francisco," Angie demanded.

"Yes, sir, it will be there in fifteen minutes," the male voice replied.

"Patch me through to Colonel Weaver," Angie asked.

She waited not more than ten seconds before Colonel Weaver was on the line.

After listening to him for a few moments, she said, "set up the defense in the bay, below the San Francisco Bridge. We've got them, now. That's the only way out to open sea. I'll be there in less than an hour."

The helicopter was already in site from the boat by the time Angie got off the phone. Stripping off his wet suit, Lucky prepared to go with Duncan and Angie as they boarded the helicopter for the nearest airport. They were taken to the John Wayne Airport and immediately boarded a plane for San Francisco. On the plane they received the details of the third attack.

A group of boaters and swimmers in the Delta near Martinque were attacked. It was estimated that twenty-eight people were either killed or mutilated. During this attack, the sharks actually attacked the smaller boats and windsurfers cruising across the water.

By the time the group had landed at the San Francisco Airport, the fleet of boats had lined up under the San Francisco Bridge. Large nets where draped from the San Francisco beach to the Sausalito side of the bay. The bridge itself was closed. News helicopters flew around the coast side of the Pacific, but were forbidden to enter the bay area directly before the open sea. The divers from the US Navy were already in the shark cages and sat waiting at the bottom in the frigid water of the bay. When Angie arrived at the site, she along with Lucky and Duncan were taken down to one of the boats. Lucky perused the site and said, "It looks like its Seymour time."

Duncan followed Angie below the deck. Angie started to strip so she could put on a wet suit.

"You're not going down there, are you?" Duncan asked her. It was just a few hours before she was telling him of her fears of facing the sharks again.

"I have to," she said simply.

"You don't have to do nothing," he said whispering to her so no one would hear his words even though they were alone.

"I have to do this," she said with a steel voice.

"Why, why you? After everything that's happened to you, the last thing you need is to be looking straight into the mouth of a pack of Great White sharks. And these Great Whites. We don't know what they're really capable of."

"It's my job," Angie replied.

"It's your job? It's your job?" Duncan said exasperated at this woman. Her terror had been transferred to him. "Is it your job to be killed? No one will think less of you if you don't go."

"I'll think less of me," she answered him.

"I don't want you to go," Duncan said at last.

Angie smiled at him.

"Thanks," she said before she zipped up her wet suit. She did not look at him again as she walked up the stairs to the deck. She entered the shark cage sitting by the side of the boat. Duncan looked at Lucky already standing in the cage. Lucky seemed excited at the prospect of hand-to-hand combat with the Great Whites. Despite all of Lucky's activist views, he was still excited at the thought of meeting the sharks. Of perhaps understanding them more than he did now.

Angie disappeared along with Lucky in the shark cage as it was lowered into the murky water of the bay. The day was clear, but a strong wind from the Northwest was stirring up waves. Hundreds of white foam waves covered the surface of the San Francisco Bay. Duncan did not take his eyes off of Angie for a moment even though she did not bother to look at him once. The moment before her eyes disappeared below the water's surface, her eyes found his. He wondered if he would ever see her again.

CHAPTER 28

3:37 *PM*:

Angie and Lucky were lowered in the shark cage to the bottom of the rocky San Francisco Bay. A line of nets fell behind them before the bay spread out to the ocean. They could see several of the other shark cages in the water. Two divers were positioned in each cage with underwater guns and spears. Lights from each of the cages glowed in the darken water. Angie's heart was beating fast. In the rush of the moment, of getting here, it was easy to be brave. But now in the eeriness of the water and as the mission loomed before her, her fear began to grip her heart. She had been in the water countless times before during her research. She had been in the shark cages before, had encountered the Great Whites many times, but this time was different. She wasn't quite sure what she was facing—or what was her biggest demon. The sharks themselves or just the fear of the sharks. Images of Stog's body being ripped apart appeared in her mind. And the fear of being left in the cold water alone with a great white circling her gripped her throat until she could hardly breath. Then came a humming. At first, Angie didn't know what it was. Then came that tune. That stupid tune that she always made fun of. Lucky was singing.

"It's Seymour, the friendly white shark, it's Seymour . . . he'll either smile at you or eat you up."

Angie turned toward Lucky to see his eyes ablaze with energy. And then fear. When Angie turned around, she could see the sharks. There was a whole pack of them and they were advancing.

CHAPTER 29

4:01 PM:

The sharks, in an aggressive stance, rushed toward the cages. Their numbers were not so great—maybe there were only twenty or thirty of them. But with creatures of that size and speed, no matter how few the numbers, the size of the advancing force was overwhelming. Each man took into his own heart his fear. The Great Whites, God's greatest creation of a pure killer, sensed their own battle. And their own survival. It was man versus nature at its basic.

Each shark weighed between 3,000 and 5,000 pounds. These were the guys Lucky was talking about. These were the guys who lived in the open ocean. Who with swift determination and calculation ruled over the ocean. These animals knew no fear. They feared nothing. These killers could cause hundreds of large whales, mammals much bigger than themselves, to beach themselves instead of living through the terror of being eaten alive. Of having your flesh torn from your body while your brain was still functioning enough to know their great power. It was like having a Mack truck aim straight for you when you were on a bicycle. The great fish had all the advantage. Humans were incapable of combating their strength and their sheer size. It was no contest.

Many of the men in the shark cages fled to the rear of their cages, as if this position would give them any advantage. One great shark after another hit the cages, throwing the occupants against the floors of the cages. The sharks seemed to work in pairs. As one shark rammed the cage, another would swim close to the cage catching any arms or legs that might fall through the bars of the cage. Soon the water was full of blood. The blood and the terrifying screams of men whose flesh was being torn from their bodies, made those men who remained unharmed act against orders. One man thought his only chance was to swim to the surface. To try somehow to get to a boat. As his black-lined body swam to the surface, he was quickly eaten whole by one of the bigger sharks. Two or three other men tried the same and they too were quickly torn apart by the pack of sharks. The sharks swam around without any routine in a frenzy ramming the cages. It was impossible to see anything.

Angie, who had been knocked down to the bottom of the cage when a shark hit them, had her leg sticking out between the bars. She tried to pull her leg inside the cage, but her flipper was caught and would not allow her to pull her leg into the safety of the cage. A Great White was rushing her cage from the side. It was only at the last moment she was able to pull her foot to safety as the shark, with its open mouth, passed within inches of her foot.

For several minutes, Angie was unable to come to grips with the situation. She could see the men around her as they fled toward the surface. And the arms and legs of others being bitten off. All her lifetime of fears came down to this reality. She was going to die, as she feared she would die—in the mouth of a Great White. She could not see any way out of it.

At first the sharks attacked the cages, but then a few headed out toward the open sea. But the large nets caught them. A panic set in with the sharks. They were in a frenzy of activity throwing their mighty weight against the nets. One was caught and was flipped upside down. His comrades soon started eating the flesh of his body. He was soon nothing but bits of chewed tissue. More sharks became entangled in the nets. Others lashed out at the captured sharks biting bits of their flesh off. The sharks seemed to turn on each other in their fear.

It was Lucky who noticed the sharks getting caught in the nets. As they flipped and rolled around for their very survival, Lucky was the first to use the spear gun. When the first shot hit his intended victim, he was hooked on the kill. With no less malicious intent than that first Great White shark attacking the surfers off the Santa Barbara coast, Lucky attacked the sharks.

The surviving divers soon followed his lead. It was their drive to survive, a drive no less or more than that of the sharks they fought, which drove the men to viciously attack their prey. The divers, who had remained in the cage, saw the tide of fear turning. Gathering their wits they started to attack the sharks using their underwater guns and spears.

Shark after shark was killed, a victim of the nets and the guns and spears of the men and of their own comrades. The water was the color of streaked blood—that of both men and sharks.

Finally, a quiet settled in the water under the bay. The sand, which had been stirred up during the fight, again settled on the floor of the bay. The surviving men were lifted in their cages to the boats.

CHAPTER 30

4:46 **PM**:

When Angie's cage was pulled up to the boat, she did not notice Duncan as he waited for her. Her interest was in her victory.

Duncan ran toward Angie as she stepped out of the cage. Her face was hard with emotion and determination.

"Angie, Angie," he found himself calling the woman he loved. "Are you alright? What happened down there?"

Angie looked at him strangely as if she didn't understand what language he spoke. She didn't have any time for him now. Not with her prey laying on the deck of the boat.

One of the dead sharks was being lifted onto the deck of the boat. Angie watched as the great fish was flipped onto the boat. The great mountain of the shark laid there dead.

"Angie, what happened to you down there?" Duncan asked her as he grabbed her wet body. He hardly noticed the great creature lying on the deck.

"Everything," she answered as she looked at the shark. Then she smiled at Duncan showing her teeth.

"We won."

She went over to look at the dead shark lying on its back with its great belly lying exposed. Like a victorious warrior that she was, she ran over to the shark and with her knife started to cut open the shark's massive belly. As she cut through the thick flesh she felt like she was releasing all of her fears. When she cut it open, her hands reached down to pull out the guts of the shark. Then something made her stop. The stomach of the shark spilled out several baby sharks, not more than one or two feet long. The small sharks were still alive and flipped around of the deck of the boat. One of the baby sharks caught hold of a sailor's leg before it was savagely beaten to death. The sailor had a serious wound. Both Angie and Duncan watched in silence, along with the rest of the crew, as the small sharks died, one by one, on the deck of that boat. Angie was both victorious and ashamed of her revenge.

CHAPTER 31

5:07 PM:

Lucky had been watching Angie cut open the shark with the rest of the crew. The struggling baby sharks squirmed around on the deck. After a few moments, he went below. Angie noticed Lucky as he walked toward the stairs leading to the cabin. His face showed his sorrow.

"He was the one who saved us," Angie said to Duncan.

"What do you mean?" Duncan asked her.

"I panicked. He was the one who started killing the sharks."

"Lucky?" Duncan asked as he saw Lucky's back disappear into the cabin.

"Yea, Lucky. It was horrible down there," she began to tell Duncan. "At first I panicked. I think we all panicked. It was unbelievable how they came in force. They were like an army. An undefeatable army. I thought I was dead. I was sure of it. And then Lucky started killing them. Once they started getting tangled in the nets it was all over for them."

"Do you think you got them all?" Duncan asked her.

"I don't know," Angie said as she looked west toward the open waters of the Pacific Ocean. "I don't know."

CHAPTER 32

3:29 PM:

Near Morrow Bay in the middle of the California coast, there is an inlet, hidden from the rough Pacific Ocean by a long strip of land. A lone wounded shark entered the mouth of the inlet and swam to the shallow waters. The shark was seriously wounded with a gunshot wound to its hindquarters. The shark had managed to swim the 70 miles or so in less than a day, leaving behind it a trail of blood. Only because of its determination did the prehistoric animal make it to this small, tranquil body of water. It was in this water that the shark had been born and instinct bought her back. In a small cove of the inlet, the shark gave birth to several baby sharks. An hour later she died after she again had swum out into the open water of the ocean. Small bull sharks devoured her body. The baby sharks, eight in number, swam toward the open sea but not before one of the larger baby sharks ate one of its smaller brothers.

And the evolution of life continues . . .